Derry's Vampire

By Bill Morris

○ ☾ ☆

New ○ Sun Publications

Half Moon Bay, California

Dedication

To love lost and come again.

Bill Morris

Our love stays there

Stubborn as a mule

Lively as desire

Cruel as memory

Stupid as regrets

Tender as remembrances

Cold as marble

Beautiful as the day

Fragile as a child

Jacques Prevert

Cet Amour, *Paroles*

United Airlines 727 pilot,

"Roger Tower, ready and waiting."

The Loss

Chapter 1

My name is Bill. I am a vampire killer.

Chapter 2

I had tracked her for two days. As she walked through the park, her long yellow hair swinging off her shoulders like wings, she looked distracted. I kept my pace a hundred yards behind her, matching her progress as she stepped along looking at her feet. She was heavy in thought. I knew why she was disturbed.

Her concentration was such that she didn't see the three men in dirty shirts and low-hanging pants step out of the bushes ahead of her and wait. They folded their arms across their chests gang-member style watching their victim step unaware into their grasp. It was a secluded back area of the park, a woodsy dell, with a wall of thick brush to pull

1

victims behind. An area that brings out the possibility of crime in base hearts.

I picked up my steps.

She was full figured, dressed in white T shirt and bright yellow shorts. I could see why the three men would accost her. The front of her shirt said "Love Up" complete with a winged heart on her chest.

She didn't even look up until one of the men said something. Then she stopped and stepped back abruptly. They must have said something pretty rude. One of her hands went from her hip to the top of her chest as she stepped back.

The three men stepped forward with arms out.

She back-pedaled fast, turned to run, when one man with an old blue bandanna on his head reached and caught her elbow.

There was a brief tug of war. Then the three surrounded her and escorted her into the bushes. The bush kind of wagged like an old woman mournfully shaking her head after the jostling party disappeared.

I started jogging to get to Derry.

I decided I wouldn't kill these three.

That would upset Derry too much to make her trust me.

Chapter 3

When I pushed through the brush and sighted the group, I saw one man holding Derry from behind, pinning her arms back, and the one in blue bandanna ripping her T-shirt away. The shirt came apart stretching like dough. Derry went to scream, but the one holding her clamped his hand over her mouth. Her breasts were large and shaking and the other two men were commenting. Derry was struggling, blinking and looking around desperately. She kicked out, missing.

The one pinning Derry laughed.

Blue Bandanna, with oily hair that was rust red, gave Derry a quick cuff on the cheek. He had well-rounded shoulders like those of a weight-lifter that bulged under a gray T-shirt. He was reaching down to undo his slouching pants.

"Hey, who wants to die today?" I called cheerfully.

The three men looked at me. I picked my way into their bushy hiding spot. Their faces were masks of surprise as I interrupted their play.

Blue bandanna crouched, went to his pocket, pulled out a knife.

The one holding Derry gave her a violent shake that bucked her head sideways and jerked her like a shield in my direction.

"Help me," Derry gasped.

"Get outa here or I'll cut you," said the one with the knife. He was holding it up like a candle for me to see its steel flame.

"This is going to be fun," I said.

3

So I got down to business. I'm pretty efficient at it. As a vampire killer I've had years of practice.

I stepped up to the one with the blue bandanna, and as he lifted his blade toward me, preparing to lunge, I hit him in the side of the face with my cane.

Then I took his knife away.

Then I punched him in the head so hard he rolled over when he hit the ground.

Derry was now yelling for help with full lungs.

I turned. The other two idiots were nearly out of sight, scrambling for escape. They hadn't liked what they'd seen.

My blood was up, and I bent down to jam my cane through Blue Bandanna's chest, when I checked myself. I didn't want to irreparably scare Derry.

I stepped back to give my grounded victim room. He crawled then stumbled blinking in pain after his departing friends.

I walked over to Derry who was now trying unsuccessfully to cover her chest before me.

"Are you all right?" I asked. My voice was a bit raspy with emotion, which Derry mistook as concern for her, but was really me trying to swallow back my need to kill. I don't let many go once I have them on the ground.

Derry turned her back for privacy and nodded yes.

"I can't go anywhere," she said, "like this."

"No, we can't," I said and handed her my black leather jacket.

Chapter 4

I walked Derry out of the brush into the open sunlight and grassy park grounds. Derry was furtively pulling her fingers through her hair and holding the jacket closed at her chest. Trying to pull her composure back together.

I asked Derry her name.

"Derry St. George," she said to the air before her.

Then as if she'd woken up, she looked at me.

"And yours?"

"Bill. Bill Mauler. Glad to meet you, Derry. Even under such sorry circumstances. Shall I go call the police?" I said.

"Thanks for helping me, Bill," said Derry. She gave me a look that said she meant it. Her eyes were royal blue.

"Many wouldn't," she said.

I nodded.

"You seemed to know what you were doing back there," said Derry.

"Retired military," I lied.

"Lucky for me. What branch of the military?"

"Intelligence and extra-curricular activities," I said.

"And so you don't want to talk about it," said Derry finishing my sentence.

I smiled and shrugged.

"Well, thank you anyway for your help."

"Shall we call the police?" I asked again helpfully.

Derry gave a solemn shake of her head.

"No. It wouldn't do any good. The police already know about me well enough. They won't want to believe or deal with me. They just kind of want to clean up the garbage after a wreck and chase fleeing criminals. They don't prevent anything. If you can't prove it, it isn't a crime."

Derry sighed. I could see her distraction flooding back in her face.

"Why do you say the police know about you?" I asked.

"In recent months I've been to them enough that they secretly refer to me as the Vampire woman."

"Are you a vampire, Derry?" I asked with just the right lilt of skepticism.

"No, I'm not."

Derry took a cool look around the boundaries of the sunny park that I had tracked her to in my quest. My quest to kill the biggest vampire. She shook her head, as if mocking herself for what she was about to say to a total stranger.

"It's just that recently, Bill, I've come to believe in them."

Chapter 5

As I looked on Derry, her chin began to quiver.

Then her face broke up and she cried.

Chapter 6

I could see her standing there in the middle of the big city park, feeling the loneliness, helplessness, and despair that the sunlight of city parks can bring to some people. Surrounded by crowds of people that didn't know or understand you, the isolation was like standing in a crowd with an invisible shower curtain pulled around you, so that even as you wept people could safely walk by without seeing you.

"Derry, would you like to go sit down on that bench and talk?" I offered. I waved a hand like a policeman beckoning traffic.

"I don't want to take up your time. You've been more than kind enough."

"I have nothing but time," I said and meant it.

"Come on, sit down," I said, "Tell me about your vampires."

Chapter 7

We sat on a bench together in a private corner of the park. As Derry wiped at her eyes to pull the last tears like makeup over her cheeks, she looked sideways and attempted a smile.

"I must look a sight," she muttered.

I shrugged.

The park bench where we sat was surrounded by an jungle of flowers, red tulip beds staunch with discipline, lazy blue petunias lounging lizard-like along sidewalks, red gladiolas sending up their red rockets like bursting fireworks, and over a high surrounding fence crept the viney searching cargo nets of red passion flowers. Sidewalks were white and hot, the air clean. I took in a deep breath, decompressing from my little exertion with Derry's attackers.

"Nice here," I said.

Derry blinked and looked. "It's hard for me to even see flowers, I've been so worried lately."

"That happens," I said.

An orange and black Monarch came in wagging and zig-zagging around Derry's yellow shorts. It hung in there fluttering, not moving on.

As I watched, Derry put out her finger and the butterfly landed on it.

I laughed, first at the incongruity of seeing this little act of nature, delicate and unthought of, when my whole focus was ramming sharpened stakes through the hearts of gasping vampires. Second, at the recognition of the potential for feeling of a person who would think of doing such a thing: offering a momentary perch for a butterfly.

I knew I was sitting next to someone.

Chapter 8

"So tell me," I said, hunching my shoulders in invitation.

Derry looked over and gave me a smile that was more than half grimace.

"It concerns my son, who's five. Though I suppose there's not much you can do about it. The police have done nothing."

"I can listen," I said.

Derry's face brightened a shade from pain to doubtful appreciation and she nodded.

"What about your son?" I coaxed.

"About a year and a half ago, I think my son was bitten by a vampire." Derry sucked in her breath and glanced aside for any gesture or look of cynicism from me. Stoically, I nodded for her to go on.

"Why do you think it was a vampire?"

"Well, it was an ugly and confusing incident. And I'm still recovering from it, so is my son. It also destroyed my marriage." Derry had said this last as a small matter of fact.

"What happened?"

I knew only the most general things about her son's attack. I was keenly interested to learn the details.

"One night, someone entered our house. My husband and I were asleep, and this person entered my son's room while he slept. There was a window on the alley way, and we had mistakenly left it open a crack. I never heard anything. But this person came in and attacked my son."

Derry drew in air with the telling of this story.

"Was your son badly hurt?" I asked.

Derry shook her head.

"No, no. He seemed fine. We heard a scream in the dark house, and my husband and I put on the lights and rushed down to his room. And..."

Derry's lips pursed.

I let her sit in silence a few seconds until she was ready.

"And when we came into his room, there was a dead old man at the foot of my son's bed."

"Dead?" I asked.

"Yes."

"Had he hurt your son before he died?" I asked.

"No," said Derry, "My son was sitting up in bed, wide-eyed, and he said the man had tried to eat him."

Chapter 9

"But your son wasn't hurt?" I asked again.

"No. It didn't appear so. We called the police, and they came out and discovered the body in my son's room. They asked us questions. They acted as if we'd made a big mistake by leaving the window open. Almost implying we'd helped commit the crime. As if the window were the problem, and I guess it was."

"But really, the fact that a man crawled inside my son's window and died in his room, that was just another interesting fact in their police lives, a grand note in their criminal diaries: The Time When That Old Man Died in That Kid's Room, you know? " said Derry, her lips nearly sneering, "And since my son didn't appear to be hurt, they asked a few more questions and cleaned up the mess, hauled the dead body out in a bag to an ambulance, and left for the next crime scene, like leaving for the next party in a progressive dinner."

"It was offensively simple," concluded Derry.

"Derry, did they ever tell you why the man died?"

"The coroner's assistant who loaded the bag just said it looked like old age. The man was just skin and bones in his clothes. And tremendously old. He was just an evil looking skull head and thin bony arms and legs inside these raggedy old clothes."

"And your son was okay?" I asked.

"Yes, he seemed to be, but then slowly, he became quite sickly. His eyes blackened, and steadily in the weeks to follow, there were many little illnesses. He became listless. I don't know. The illnesses were unspecific and small. Passing. But my son, he was sick. It was like his spirit was withering."

"Did you see a doctor about it?"

"Oh, yes, but the doctor seemed confused. He gave my son medicines for six different diseases. From mononucleosis, hepatitis, to TB. I knew he was just guessing. And the whole time, I knew. "

Derry blinked back tears for several seconds.

"What did you know, Derry?" I asked.

Derry sniffed. She looked straight ahead in the air.

"I knew that old man was a vampire."

Chapter 10

"How do you know that?" I asked.

"I don't know, I don't know. I can't tell you. I just know. My son was attacked by a vampire. And now he's...still in danger."

I didn't ask Derry to explain this. I knew it was utterly true.

Chapter 11

"I went to the police. I told them what I thought. I told them I needed to know more about this old man. They just looked at each other as if saying, 'Here's another one for the books: *She wants us to investigate a dead old man to see if he was a vampire*.' I was just another crazy victim to them. Crazy because something unexplained, unexpected had happened to me. And now I wanted my world put right again. But I may as well have asked them to admit they were powerless oafs addicted to the chase. They're just garbage men really."

Derry's bitterness was so deep you could almost drink it with pleasure.

"So, now I'm the crazy vampire woman. And they cringe when they see me, and they're doing nothing."

Derry paused.

"Do you think I'm crazy?"

"Craziness is in the eyes of the beholder," I said. "It can also mean you've seen the horror of the real thing."

"I've seen it," said Derry firmly.

"I believe you have," I said.

I smiled to confirm a new-found friendship.

Chapter 12

The park flowers around us in the mid-day sun seemed to be ringing with color. I could see a light sweat forming on Derry's neck as she sat hunched in my black leather coat telling her story.

"What about your husband, what does he think?" I asked.

Derry shrugged.

"I don't really care what he thinks, actually."

I tilted my head to signal I didn't understand.

"Oh, he left me a few months later. He went off on a business trip to sleep with his new secretary and never came back. Meanwhile my son is getting sicker and sicker. And that ass leaves me. Within a month, I'm getting divorce papers in the mail. The divorce became final yesterday. I... I just can't believe it."

"Why did he leave you? At such a time of trouble?"

"I don't know. I don't know!" Derry said. I could see the trembling enter her face again. Frustration and helplessness imminently ready to overwhelm her.

I could guess why he'd left her: it was vampires piling it on.

"So you have custody of your child? Could I talk to him?"

"No one can see him. Not my husband, not you, not anyone. Not until I get this vampire business taken care of somehow. I've hidden him, and the judge can throw me in jail. I don't care. No one is seeing him. Not until I know what to do."

"Why hide him?" I asked.

Derry's chin rose, which I mistook as an instant for pride, but it actually meant she didn't care what anyone thought about it.

"Because, I think he still may be in danger from other vampires. So he'll stay hidden until I know what's going on."

Chapter 13

"Perhaps I could help you in some way?" I asked.

Derry looked over at me with an appraising eye.

"Why? How?"

"I could look into it for you. I could check things out."

"As for why, well, because I want to. It calls upon my past experience, so to speak. We'll just have to leave it at that."

"Why would you help me when we've just met?"

"I began helping you even before we met," I reminded her pleasantly. "Who else is offering to help you with your vampires?"

"No one," admitted Derry.

"And we must be friends: you're already wearing my clothes," I said, pointing my chin at the jacket.

Derry looked down at my leather jacket, heavy and hot on her shoulders, and nodded good-naturedly at my joke.

"You mean you'd investigate for me? You're some sort of a private-eye or something?"

"No," I said with a sad shake of my head, "I'm not a private investigator, nothing like that. I don't investigate, that's too elevated a term for what I do...Let's just say I hunt. "

Derry looked at me in silence.

Then I told her the absolute truth.

"I hunt people and other things."

And, what I didn't say, when I found these *other things* I killed them and laughed in the face of their agony.

Chapter 14

"Look," I said, "Let's continue talking. But first, let's get you out of that jacket into a change of clothes."

"Okay. I don't live far from here," said Derry.

"And after we get you out of that hot jacket, we'll do the first most important thing in our hunt for vampires," I said.

"What's that?" asked Derry.

"We'll have lunch."

Chapter 15

There are a variety of ways in which you can kill a vampire. I stick to three mainly. To do it safely, the first rule is that you must not engage with vampires with any high emotions. For then they can feed upon these emotions and get stronger. If they can run your emotions high enough, then you become weary, and vampires can overcome you. So, when you go to kill a vampire cold-bloodedness is essential. You should get no thrill of horror or delight as a struggling vampire fish-wiggles on the end of your stake that you've jammed through his heart. For there goes you but for one ignorant bite. The vampire disease passes on so easily.

Though I know I look odd in modern day society, I always carry my wooden walking stick with sharp silver tip. This is my first method of dispatch. I have no limp and walk perfectly fine, so most people take it as a sign of pretension. Kind-hearted people might comment that it makes me look dapper. But in effect, it is simply a workman's tool I must keep close. Vampires see it and immediately suspect its dangers. They see the long wooden stake, the silver tip, and "see the point."

The rubber hand-grip that I've lately applied a third down the staff might give away the secret of my walking stick to any initiated. But the world is basically blind to vampires, those dark animals among us secretly sucking the emotional blood from us day in day out; the best our society sees is usually only the worst criminals.

One thing I like about my cane, its handle is a carefully carved dog's head with a laughing doggy face. I enjoy it as a kind of a good joke on me and my vampire-victims coming from this death-weapon. My cane is especially stout oak. I have literally jammed it through the wall of a bathroom stall, completely through the body of an unsuspecting vampire doing number 1, and through the opposite wall of the toilet stall next. He kicked a bit then slumped and hung there like an old coat. My stout vampire-killer staff held up magnificently. It barely bent under the dead weight of this skewered vampire. And it took quite a pull to retrieve it, dropping the now dead vampire into the privacy of his bathroom tomb like a flour sack.

Fortunately, when you kill vampires this way, vampires have no blood of their own. Otherwise when you retrieved the cane it would be a big mess. But my trusty stake always pulls out clean. Completely clean.

And as I smile down on it, the dog handle just keeps laughing.

Chapter 16

"Why do you carry a cane? You don't seem to limp. Did you injure your leg?" asked Derry as we strolled to the edge of the park.

"I have a problem with my inner ear and sense of balance."

"What do you do for a living?"

"Retired. I have a lot of time on my hands," I said.

"You seem quite young for being retired," said Derry. She was now looking my way inspecting my face for a closer look at her rescuer.

"Young? I'm practically ageless. You know the military," I lied, "You retire early then start a whole new career. Except, it's kind of hard to start a new career when basically all you know is how to kill people."

Instead of lying, I like to think of myself as dissembling. Like one of my ancient loves, poetry, when I dissemble, I think of myself as trying to reveal the truth by using a close metaphor, describing things other than they are to reveal them.

We stopped at a crosswalk waiting for the red to go green. Cars were passing back and forth in the daily confusion of traffic. At the edge of the park, haggard people in heavy backpacks traipsed along the sidewalk, slump-shouldered, as if they just climbed out from a bedroom under a bush. Other jetting and twisting people, in-line skaters in shorts and crash-helmets, were curving and zig-zagging crazily on the park sidewalk, as if driven by unseen demons. An old woman standing by a cement fountain, long dry, was throwing down rugs of seeds for ravenous pigeons. I put my hands in my pockets, one more among the menagerie.

"You seemed quite athletic back there," said Derry. "Lucky for me."

"Actually, I've been in that situation a lot more times than those three had," I said. "Once I saw them pull you into the bushes, well, I nearly made them my victims."

I said this last with the slightest accent of regret.

Derry mistook this for me expressing remorse for a former bloodthirsty lifestyle.

"I'm grateful, Bill," she said turning and putting her palm on my arm.

I looked at her and dipped my head in acknowledgment.

My regret had actually been that I was restrained and hadn't gotten to kill all three.

Red went to green.

Derry and I crossed the street toward her home.

Chapter 17

My second method of dispatching vampires is with a squirt gun. It's one of those neon-orange plastic jobs that kids use. I've tried different kinds, but the one I favor is shaped like the old military 45-automatic. It holds up to about 50 squirts. That's about forty-five vampires I might grease in a night if I didn't miss much. (I rarely kill more than two or three in a single day.)

But I'm packing big heat in my little plastic squirt gun.

As a safety, I keep a little patch of duct tape over the nozzle so that none of the load might get out and drip on me. I only pull off the duct tape from the muzzle just before I pounce.

I even keep my orange squirt gun in a little holster under my arm. (Except the holster is lined with a plastic bag...you can't be too cautious about getting this stuff on you during a hunt.)

I remember the first time I tried out the gun.

I was walking down a deserted alley at sunset, a lonesome landscape of fading light in the big city.

From out behind a blue dumpster stepped a large man with long black hair to his shoulders. He looked to be a Native American, with strong-brows and high-cheeks, except for his skin held a yellow pallor. I recognized that he had succumbed to another vampire. But he was Frankenstein size. He had big gorilla shoulders.

I nodded, "Hi."

He placed himself malevolently directly in my path. His eyes were yellow tiger's eyes.

Man, there was a lot of built-up hate there.

(Unfortunately, as any fourth grader in California who has had social studies can tell you, all that built-up hate from my Indian-vampire friend was completely justified.)

He pulled out a gun and pointed it at my chest.

I could see from a haggard look under his eyes, this big American was into drugs. He may not have even realized he was a vampire yet. (When first converted, new vampires are often confused about it.) This one probably thought all he wanted was my money.

"Give me your wallet or I kill you," he said. He swallowed a bit nervous after he said it.

I pulled out my squirt gun and pointed it at him.

The Indian was surprised. He realized he'd been slow and that when I'd reached under my shoulder he should have fired. But now, looking at me, he saw I was pointing a mere orange squirt gun between his eyes.

21

This struck him funny. He put back his head, his black hair flowing and shaking, and belly laughed with all his might. He could barely hold his own pistol in my direction. He was howling with laughter.

White men had even taken to killing Indians with squirt guns.

So when I squeezed the trigger, shooting some of my bitter poison into his laughing mouth, he was again entirely surprised as his soul fried and left him.

He dropped like a poleaxed steer.

I sighed with satisfaction.

As a vampire-killer I realized I had the right weapon.

Chapter 18

You're wondering what it is that I put in my squirt gun. It's a secret elixir of mine that is basically water. I simply put in a few drops of a rare ingredient, one so toxic to vampires that it kills them dead even when I dilute a single drop in a gallon of water.

So man, am I ever careful when I mix up a batch of squirt gun ammo. I don a heavy plastic butcher-shop apron, thick rubber gloves up to my elbows, and wear a welder's mask as I take tweezers and tip a thimble over the mouth of a five-gallon water jug. The thimble usually only contains two drops of a clear clear liquid.

The liquid is simply a child's tears.

22

Chapter 19

After a few more minutes of strolling city sidewalks away from the park, we stopped before Derry's apartment building. It was an extremely old building, four stories of ocher cement blocks, covered in a joyous tower of pink flowering clematis. The building seemed designed just to hold up the viney wall of flowers, reaching skyward like praise toward heaven.

It was quite a facade.

"You live here?" I asked, "It's a beautiful building."

"Yes. I fell in love with the sight of those flowers. I just moved in. I'd lived in an old house down farther by the park. But I moved here, since the divorce."

"You're selling your house because of the divorce?"

"No," said Derry. Then she hesitated.

"Why did you move then?"

"I'm hoping it's a safer location."

Derry looked around her, rubbing her hands, hesitating before going up the front steps. She looked at me and then looked away.

I realized she was worried about bringing me, a stranger, into her apartment building. I could understand that. No use tempting fate twice in a day.

"I'll wait here while you change," I said. "You can just bring the jacket down."

Derry flashed a smile that would melt ice cream.

"Thanks, Bill," she said and turned and trotted up the stairs, clutching at the bottom of the jacket as she ran, heading for the safety of her front door.

I sat down on the first stair and waited, my cane across my lap, like any gargoyle sentry.

Chapter 20

My third method of killing vampires I only use when I expect to be facing many at once. I use it when I don't expect to be killing vampires in especially close quarters. It's such a dangerous weapon I have to be careful that it doesn't splash back on me. But when I want to kill a lot of vampires fast, I pick up my Big Squirt 2000.

The Big Squirt 2000 has big water bulbs on the stock and barrel, flamboyant lime green, that hold about two liters of water. One of those pump water pistols, shaped like a tommy gun, it'll shoot a string of water about 25 ft. It's surprisingly accurate. Because it holds a big load and fires both in bursts and continuously, I can use it to mow down vampires left and right.

The first time I used it was against *Los Vampiros* , a street gang in Long Beach. You know, the kind of gang where members have gang names like Happy, Doc, Creepy, Sneezey, Dopey, Cheetos and Tupper (as in Tupperware.) Sure, I'm being facetious; but these gang members were not. They were vampires of a particularly heinous kind. They were young men addicted to feeding solely off the lower dark feelings of humiliation, frustration, vexation, anger, despair. Some vampires, of course, feed off the higher emotions of love, trust, even admiration and approval found in their victims. But this city gang, used to poverty, lived solely with their black vision focused on the wrongs done them, revenge, and sucking up surrounding hate.

Many fed on children in the schoolyards and local neighborhood, recruiting ever growing numbers for the gang. But because vampire gang members are poor in emotions, there of course isn't enough to go around, which naturally leads to territoriality and warfare. For vampire gangs, the best place to find hate is in the hearts of other gangs. So in the Long Beach barrio, the *Vampiros* preyed upon other gangs, the Crips, the Bloods, swooping in for bloodletting, hate-sprees, drive-by-orgies of bloodlust. And, of course, the jollies afforded by an occasional gang rape.

It was such a gang rape that led to my buying the Big Squirt 2000 and wiping the gang from the face of the earth. A shiver of happiness goes through me just to think of it.

I was staying overnight in downtown Long Beach at the Mariott Heritage. Down town Long Beach in the late evening sunset is graceful, clean, with leaning palm trees and a distant view of the working harbor. I was returning from a kill in San Diego and stopped for the night on my return route to San Francisco. I'd picked up a local paper, the Long Beach Foghorn, to find an article about *Los Vampiros*. Only a few blocks from my hotel they had grabbed a young Latina girl, (name withheld), 11 years old, and six of the gang had taken her to an alley. In the alley, one gang member (with shaven skull according to the recount), sat on the girl's head while the others took turns raping.

Something in this froze my blood. It was because my daughter was 11 when she was killed.

But as I looked in the mirror, strapping on my trusty orange 45 squirt, I frowned. It didn't seem adequate for such a job.

So I went out to a local 5 & 10 and bought the Big Squirt 2000.

Then I went back to my room and mixed up a big batch of vampire-icide.

The poverty, graffiti, broken windows, and poor housing conditions begin a few blocks away from down town Long Beach. As you drive, you see the bobbing grasshopper heads of the big oil pumps pecking at the earth behind people's backyards. You know as these pumps gracefully nod, sucking the abundant blackness from the earth, not a nickel of it goes back into the Latino community.

I asked an old man in my halting Spanish were I could find the *Vampiros*. His head up with pride and suspicion, he merely pointed to a vacant lot and slow-nodding oil pumps a few blocks away.

I said *gracias* and drove in that direction.

The lair of the *Vampiros* was a big lot surrounded by a broken down cyclone fence, embracing a small metropolis of dented oil drums, winch equipment, and a Texaco oil pump long stilled like a museum dinosaur. Deposited randomly around the rusting metal and drums were lounging Latino gang members, roughly 14 to 21 years old. They were slouching here and there kind of like mannequins modeling old clothes in a castaway shop. A few shiny cars in candy colors, of old vintage, but well-kept, squatted on their low-rider wheels at the curbside. A spaghetti of black graffiti was scribbled on everything flat, including the sidewalk.

26

Heads with bandannas and backward-faced baseball caps turned my way as I parked. Several youths in thick and drooping flannel shirts cocked their heads to look at me from their sentry positions at a broken down opening in the fence.

As I got out of my car and looked at them over the hood, I saw about 12 young men getting to their feet.

The evening's entertainment had arrived.

"I'm looking for the *Vampiros*," I shouted in cheery voice.

I have to say the death-joy had entered my heart.

A very sullen young man with menacing scowl, bulldog neck, and pig-shaved skull came marching toward me out of the oil junkyard.

"Whatchu want the *Vampiros* for, cabrone?" he challenged.

"Just a minute, Cheetos," I said, holding up a finger. I went back in my car and came up porting the Big Squirt 2000, pointed safely at the sky.

My bald companion flinched as I came up with what looked like a weapon. Then seeing it was a squirt gun, he relaxed, and crossed his arms at his chest with a haughty grimace.

"Whatchu going to do with that piece of plastic?" he asked.

I said slowly, "I'm going to kill you all."

This made Cheetos laugh. He motioned to his fellows which shortly brought a small crowd to the side of my car. Even a little white gang dog, a scruffy pitbull, came up and looked at me inquiringly.

"This man, he's going to execute us with that squirt gun," cried Cheetos to his gang.

"What's in it?" said another voice from the group.

"Just a little water and baby's tears," I said. I squirted the sidewalk a bit at the dog's feet. The dog took an investigative sniff, then ever-thirsty, took an experimental lapping taste. The white pitbull looked up, tongue out, happy.

"So, you're going to kill us with that?" asked Cheetos.

"Yes."

Cheetos looked around as if to share the gag with his compatriots. "Well, cabrone, you can execute us. Then, we will execute you, our style."

I smiled. "I like your logic. Let's do it. Who's first?"

Cheetos obliged by ordering all his gang-members to form up in a line, with him standing bold and ready at the front for the first squirt. The gang moved into position, hands at sides like men against a wall, with an attitude of showing their toughness to the world by being ready to take a shot without flinching.

"Fire away, then we play," sneered Cheetos.

I raised the Big Squirt 2000 and pulled the trigger. I walked carefully down the line splashing each gang member in the face. Cooperatively they didn't flinch. At least for the first second or two.

Then as they began to grab their faces, stagger, fall to their knees, they fell like dominoes. Cheetos was screaming and shaking his head as if being electrocuted. And as the vampire gang sank to the ground, writhing in agony, one falling upon the other, their basic animal instincts took over. Blinded, dying in a pile, unconscious of what had killed them, the vampires began flailing and fighting each other.

In a few seconds, they were all dead.

I was extremely pleased with the effect.

Chapter 21

I heard a click behind me and turned to see the front door of Derry's apartment building open and Derry's head appear with a bouquet tied to her hair. Actually it was three white gardenias knotted to a pony-tail strangely pulled from above her ear. Derry looked down on me smiling with a tilted head, finding me looking at her with back turned.

"Well, you're still here," called Derry with mock-dismay.

"Lucky you," I said.

Derry descended the steps with a curvaceous walk, a model descending the runway, my black jacket thrown in a casual lump over her shoulder. She wore a sleeveless summer dress in white and yellow florals that billowed like tissue curtains in wind. The dress was cinched around her waist with a small yellow cord, the type you might see laid across an open Bible. Her legs were bare with glossy yellow low-heeled shoes that had two twisting snake straps that crossed her feet up to her ankles. She was young, healthy, and smiling, as she walked to me with welcome in her eyes.

I'm not the kind to fall down and worship at the feet of the Diva.

But then again, maybe.

"We still having lunch?" asked Derry as I rose. She tossed the black jacket into my chest and I caught it.

"Definitely," I said. "Now you're here."

I told her I knew a place where we could go, not far from the park. So we set off walking again, this time I noticed with an extra few inches between us.

Derry playfully asked to try out walking with my stick.

And I let her.

Chapter 22

Of course, there's a big difference between when I kill a vampire with my walking stick and when I get it with a squirt.

You see, when I skewer a vampire with my stick, it doesn't kill the vampire's soul. It only kills the vampire's body. The soul is free to migrate to another body on the next incarnation. The vampire has a chance to become human again. I usually only do this with fresh-made vampires, those who haven't done much damage in their short vampire lives. Though I kill them young, when they are still confused about their nature, ignorant of who they are with their malingering dark vision of sucking it out of the world, at the world's expense, I give their souls a break, and hope they will learn better the next go around. Often they were children when they were taken by the vampire that made them, often it's Mom, Dad, and family that tasted their blood and created a new vampire to join the clan. They can't help it. It's just vampire ignorance, which is profound. So I may cut them some slack. A good skewering can be a cosmic lesson, if you know what I mean.

But the worst cases, vampires of great age, cunning, or wrathfulness, those I scour their souls from the universe. I don't toy with rehabilitation for those whose shadow has cast death and destruction upon tens, hundreds, thousands, hundred thousands, even millions upon this earth. Did you know the inventor of the terrorizing VII rocket was a vampire working for his favorite people, the Germans? Vampires, especially in groups, can come up with incredibly vicious mischief.

So I give them a squirt and send their souls into oblivion.

And if they writhe around a little bit, I enjoy that too.

Chapter 23

Several minutes later, we were seated at one of those small San Franciscan cafes with five or six empty tables draped with white table cloths like unread newspapers, the kind of cafe run by an ex-hardware store owner who's now a gourmet chef and waits tables himself. On each table, a single yellow rose stood in a slender tube vase as resolute as a candle flame.

Derry grabbed the back of her thighs and scooped the dress under her as I scooted the chair in behind her.

I sat myself down and the chef, in white shirt and pants, bowed to us dealing out two menus.

He explained the preliminaries and left us to our decisions.

"Nice place, " said Derry casting an eye around.

"I live near here, so I come occasionally," I said. I had perhaps ten residences that I owned here and there about the States, mainly in the big cities, and my San Francisco loft was one of my main resting places.

"What shall we have?" asked Derry.

"Pick your meal according to your heart and let your stomach worry about it later," I said.

"Ah, Ancient Restaurant Wisdom," jeered Derry cheerfully. "What doesn't kill you makes you stronger, right Bill?"

"And what kills you makes you rot."

Derry laughed —the first of many times that meal as that damned yellow rose leaned her way like a microphone listening to every word.

Chapter 24

"What do you do with your time?" I asked Derry after we had half-eaten our repas.

"I'm the Director of a children's orphanage, The Sunnyrock Home for Children, over on Sanders. I've been there for years, maybe ten. It's a fairly large institution unfortunately for the kids. I believe kids need cozy little homes to thrive and nurture in, not classroom size walls and distantly spaced sofas and wooden desks. But I do my best to keep our little village as homelike as possible. One of my small triumphs was getting colorful rugs in each child's room. A local merchant took pity and he lets the new kids come in and pick out a rug for just themselves. It's a small thing, but having something of your own, a safely owned spot on the floor, helps keep our little keepers and throwbacks happy."

"Keepers and throwbacks?"

Derry shrugged.

"Over the years, my staff has come up with two basic labels for our many children. We have roughly 80 kids with us at any one time. All races, ages, sizes. All children sadly left to us, an orphanage cum children's village, as I like to think of it. But over the years the staff has come to see two general types of kids come through our doors. The keepers are generally younger children, still innocent or of such sweet disposition and talents that adopting families fall in love with them and take them home. The keepers are the luckies, the ones whose stay with us often for short duration. A matter of several months at most. The throwbacks, they are generally the ones destined to stay with us for years."

"Throwbacks? That sounds harsh," I said.

"No, not throwback as in Neanderthal, throwbacks as in you catch a fish you don't really want and throw it back. These are kids, generally growing older and older within the village, to whom an adopting couple will just never cross the line to make a commitment. These are children who must just stand alone in my care. They become our main population, the true tribe within our walls. Generally they are normal kids of unmet needs, although we, of course, have handicapped and mental disorders. And the sickly, we even have a small clinic and staffed nursing ward."

"The throwbacks, they are the kids who make their unmet needs known, and loudly. Their antics can be frightful and disturbing. And prospective parents are surprised and not sure they can deal with it. They'd rather start with a Tabula Rasa, a child who is a clean washed slate. But our throwbacks cannot hide what their hearts cry out for. They are thrown back because their families never supplied what they needed. And now they are thrown back precisely because they need it. So the numbers grow, and few leave, such that there is real danger of not having room for even new keepers."

"It sounds spiritually hard, your job, Derry," I said.

Derry nodded.

"Why do you do it?" I asked.

Derry gave a self-depreciating shrug.

"I was an orphan once, Bill," she said.

"But I was lucky, I was a keeper."

Chapter 25

You might wonder how I come by the secret ingredient, children's tears, that I mix with water and that kills vampires so effectively.

It's simple: I go to the newborn wards in hospitals, orphanages, even snoop around crack houses. Anywhere it's likely children are left unattended.

Chapter 26

"I'd enjoy seeing your orphanage sometime," I smiled.

"Oh, why?" asked Derry, her face brightening.

"It sounds like a better than average place."

"I've tried to make it so. I've put a lot of myself into it over the years. It's not far from here. In walking distance. That's one of the nice things. I live close by and can walk to work. The neighborhood is fairly nice, so I can even walk home late after work. One of the things I've worked on is putting in flower beds and children's park equipment so potential adopting parents aren't afraid to come in."

"I'd love to see it," I said. I was earnest.

"Maybe we can walk by after lunch. I don't normally go there on my day off. I pretty much spend six days a week there and all hours of the day working with the kids, so I make sure to take one full day off. But we could walk by. Just to see that the building's not on fire."

"Great," I said.

"Okay," said Derry happily.

"And if I like it, do you think I could move in? Do you have a room for me?"

Derry laughed.

"Sorry, you look like a throwback. No more room for those."

I laughed. Some people have an unconscious talent for making right decisions.

Derry wasn't inviting this fantastical killing machine into her orphanage.

Chapter 27

At the end of a pleasant meal, I ordered coffee for Derry and decaf for me. Odd, but I know vampires rarely drink decaf. They have to go for the caffeine. In fact, I've known vampires that get hooked on pure adrenaline. In a weird version of the extreme games, these vampires are the kind that run around jumping off rooftops and buildings onto their victims, scaring the shit out of them. Just to get that adrenaline rush.

Chapter 28

"Derry, do you mind if I ask you a question or two about the attack?"

Derry, who had been laughing at me, sobered a bit, then pushed a twig of her blond hair behind her ear, trying to order herself a bit for more serious matters.

"Sure."

"Okay," I started, "I don't know much about it, but it seems there are two odd things about this attack we should think about."

"What are those?"

"Well, your son wasn't hurt, at least it didn't appear so, in the beginning. I'd think that if an attacker or vampire enters a small child's room, in the blackness of night, it's very unlikely the child wouldn't be hurt in some way."

"Maybe he just escaped or the old man just died before he got to my son?"

"No, I don't think so."

"Why?" asked Derry.

"Because of the other odd thing. Well, I'm just guessing, but I think with vampires the victim dies so the vampire won't."

"And?" said Derry puzzled.

"And in this case something unusual happened."

"What's that?"

"The vampire died."

Chapter 29

"Here the unusual happened. Here the vampire died. The victim didn't." I sat back to look at her to see how she was taking this.

"Are you saying that somehow my five-year-old son killed this vampire?"

"I don't know, Derry," I hesitated. Then again I told her the truth.

"Maybe he did."

Chapter 30

Derry sat looking askance at me. And I realized I'd proposed something so outrageous to Derry's view that I, a very short term acquaintance, was on the edge of discrediting myself.

"I don't think five-year-olds are killers, of anything," said Derry.

"Of course not," I said smiling, "Not intentionally. But if you're sure this old man was a vampire, who I believe make their living off the blood of others, then there's nothing that should have killed him in the normal situation, with a helpless child. Yet he died, something did kill him. Let's just assume that's true. Otherwise we have to question whether he was a vampire or not. And everything you've told me is false."

"It's not," said Derry stiffly.

I paused before I went on.

"Then, Derry, we have to accept that something in this situation is outside of the normal. Something about your son killed this vampire."

We sat in silence a full minute as Derry looked away from me, slowly scanning the eating establishment, as she came to terms with what I'd said. Finally she made her decision, swallowing before she spoke to me.

"Okay, let's say somehow something about my son killed this vampire."

I inwardly smiled at Derry, admiring the courage of her mind to accept and travel toward the unknown. She really was someone.

"Then, it might be important to find out and control what that something is," I said.

"Why? Why should we try to find out and *control* it?"

"I wasn't thinking of us controlling it, Derry. I was just thinking, if it's fatal to vampires, it might be important for them to find out about it and control it." I was careful not to say *kill it*.

"So," Derry looked down at her hands, clasped together so hard her finger tips were white, "It's true. Vampires are after my son."

"Could be," I confirmed.

And it could be Derry's son had somehow created a fourth deadly way of stopping vampires, eternally dousing their bloodthirsty spirits, squashing their miserable souls like bugs under a steamroller; a fourth great way of extermination of which I could only be jealous.

Chapter 31

"Whatsay we take that walk?" I said as I rose pushing back my chair at the table.

Derry reached down for an invisible purse beside her then realized she hadn't brought one. She smiled at me.

"Where to?"

"Still want to walk me by your workplace?"

"Sure, if you want."

"Then that's that. We can talk as we walk."

I reached out and took the yellow rose from the test tube shaped vase on the table and handed it to her. She took it happily and twirled it like a small umbrella in her fingers.

I put down cash and waved good-bye to the owner as we walked out.

"Careful of thorns," I said. "They're always there."

"They're necessary, they protect the flower," Derry said, "If you see them, they're no problem."

"Yes, I suppose so," I said, my smile tight.

Chapter 33

The city streets were still bustling in mid-afternoon, cars, taxis, and grunting accelerating buses pushing fast up the tree-lined streets of the Panhandle, as if driving loads of human corpuscles to unknown destinations in the larger body.

Somehow, walking beside Derry, gardenias ribboned to her hair, with her leisurely woman's walk full of S shapes, I relaxed a bit more than normal. I almost felt as if I was strolling out of the world of vampires into the world of the ordinary.

"By the way, thanks for lunch."

"My pleasure."

"The Home is over on Sanders; we can cut through the park here. It's right on the edge of the park. About 10 minutes by foot."

"That'll be good for the digestion."

"The park is good for a lot of things, including digestion," said Derry. "People walking, leisure, flowers, a kind of garden of Eden that we can still get to. Simple goals and pleasures."

"You love the park," I said.

Derry laughed, raising her chin, closing her eyes to the sun on her face.

"I do," she said. "Among the mess of the city; the falls and tumbles, and daily turmoil of the orphanage, it's a place to reconnect."

"Reconnecting with yourself is important, if you can do it," I said.

Derry looked at me strangely hearing a faint note of regret in my voice.

"For me, it's not really reconnecting with myself so much as reconnecting to the beauty of my surroundings. I actually think when I'm busy in the bowels of the home, it's as if I'm wearing a space-helmet, packed into my own self-contained atmosphere. I can only see so far from the bubble of my own concerns. And it's in the park that I pry the fishbowl off my head, and breath in, see the garden and flowers again. Reconnect, you know?"

"Better than drugs," I said.

"Better than TV," replied Derry.

"Better than steak," I said.

"Better than chocolate turtles with pecans," Derry said.

"Better than carnival cotton candy," I said.

"Better than ice cold lemonade," replied Derry.

"Better than a hot waffle and orange juice on Sunday morning," I said.

"Better than watermelon," insisted Derry.

"Nothing," I said, shocked, "is better than watermelon."

I won. Derry laughed.

Chapter 34

After several minutes of walking, skirting meandering bicyclists roaming the sidewalk, families of all kinds walking with kids in tow like infinitely small multinational parades, and avoiding the ugly personal space of transients sitting humped here and there in the sun or under bushes like poorly-spaced garbage cans, Derry and I came to the edge of the park where the City began.

"That's the home," said Derry, pointing across yards of lawn to a two story brick building. Derry stopped, putting her hands on her hips as she gazed across the park grass.

The Sunnyrock Home for Children looked to be an old style hospital with rows of small windows along the sides. An outdated building, I guessed that it had probably been abandoned for its original purpose for lack of the immense electrical-based services of the modern day hospital. I could see trees and sidewalks around the building with an iron fence, made of upright cast iron spears set in guiding rails, surrounding the edifice. Through the fence I could see children running and jumping.

Derry motioned that we sit on a nearby park bench.

"I don't want to go too close," she said. "If they see me, they'll pull me in."

"How so?" I asked.

Derry raised her chin to the distant tribe of dancing, skipping children around the building. "Oh, lots of little bodies needing attention. They'll surround you, all struggling like a pack of hopeful puppies."

At this distance through the bars, I could see the orphanage grounds were well kept and green. Bushes lined stairwells, white rocks surrounded the base of sapling trees.

"Your grounds look pretty nice," I said.

"For an institution, you mean?" laughed Derry, "Yes, that's an area I try to keep up. Who wants to live in a home surrounded by bare dirt, concrete, and trash?"

"It was that way when you took over?" I asked.

Derry nodded.

"You've done a good job."

"Thanks. Funny though, we never seem to have flowers. I had the gardener plant dozens of kinds. But they don't last long among the crowd."

"Why?" I asked.

"Because as soon as there's a flower, it gets picked," Derry shook her head with mirth, "and nothing looks weirder than a bed of tulips standing green and tall, all with empty stems pointed toward heaven."

"The kids pick them," I said.

"Yes, they can't help it. The flowers get picked for a lot of reasons. Some kids pick them for play, others out of anger, others because they just had to have something special, some because they want to show you how wonderful that flower is so they pick it and bring it in for your approval. Flowers in the orphanage have a hard life; the needs are many and great," said Derry cheerfully.

"Naked flowers at the orphanage," I concluded.

Derry shrugged, "Sometimes, I just wish I could *make* them bloom."

Derry drew in a breath, then looked at me.

"But you can't," she said frankly. "You can't make flowers bloom."

"It's a matter of providing the right conditions," I said.

"Oh, yes," concurred Derry, "But still, you can't make flowers bloom. What makes flowers bloom is that they're free to do it."

Chapter 35

There are times when I don't feel free to do anything. Anything human that is. It's usually during the middle of the night, as I stand in my den in blackness, looking out my window at the dim bulbs and unpopulated streets of the City. I can't sleep. I just stand looking out my window. I feel an intense gnawing in my stomach. It's the intense gnawing of my anger that makes me want to kill every damn vampire I see.

It seems the only thing I'm free to do.

So, some nights, I just open my window and go out and kill one.

Chapter 36

I noticed an open area of playground equipment, swings and climbing structures at one end of the orphanage. The fierce line of spears that made up the orphanage fence had been removed to create open access to the play equipment for anyone coming down the sidewalk. Picnic tables, benches, and even a sandbox were placed invitingly among the play structures. I could see men and women, some with strollers, others standing and pushing children on swings among the groups of orphans at play. A small gate led from the little playground to the fully enclosed orphanage grounds. I could see kids running in and out at random.

"It's nice you're situated near that little playground and its equipment."

"That's actually part of the orphanage, I had it built," said Derry.

"It's not part of the Golden Gate park here?" I asked.

"No," smiled Derry, "It's the Home's equipment. I had it build as part of my advertising budget. It looks like a park, but it's really my advertising campaign."

"I don't follow," I said mystified.

"Well, Bill, you can't very well advertise orphan kids in the newspaper. But we need to attract prospective parents."

"Or else you lead the aimless life of a real estate agent waiting for buyers to walk through the office door..." I guessed aloud.

"Exactly," concurred Derry.

"So I had that little playground build. First, of course, for the kids, but then I realized if I just opened it to the public, we'd also attract families with their kids. So I took down the fence and put in the picnic tables and benches for the parents."

"But how does that advertise kids?"

"Well," said Derry, "when parents bring their kids here to play, or couples wishing for kids come by, they sometimes sit in our playground and watch the goings on. They see kids happy, they see kids lonely, they see kids crying or needing help. Often, because my kids at the home here need so much attention, the children will come up and ask questions and end up talking to the other people visiting our park. And sometimes that's all it takes to start a relationship. A little talk, a second visit where people remember each others' names and say hi. It allows potential parents and my kids the freedom to meet."

Derry laughed mischievously, "And I always hope that'll be the start of a love affair."

"You're a genius, Derry," I said.

Chapter 37

"Derry, do your kids turn out normal? When they grow up, I mean?" I asked.

"Pretty normal," said Derry, raising a hand to her brow for shade and looking out across the sunny lawn to the jumping and running kids within her orphanage playground.

"At least normal if you mean they show the whole spectrum of human behavior. I've known kids like these who grow up, struggle and make it, go to college, have a family. A few have good careers. Some spend their lives searching for things they never had as a kid. Others, the rebels push the extremes of behavior until they land in jail, become criminals. The depressed give up and turn to alcohol or drugs, even suicide. So we have the whole normal range of human outcomes." Derry blinked and looked aside at me.

"If you ask me why some end well, other badly, I don't know," said Derry, "But for those for whom it turns bad, I'd like to think it was as simple as they grew up believing love would never come."

Chapter 38

It was true for me. I knew love would never come. I no longer had the source within, the source was not in my blood. And, of course, you cannot accept from others what you can never give.

Chapter 39

A black BMW coupe with darkened windows was slowly crawling down the road in front of the orphanage. I looked over at it because Derry's head had come up when she saw it. She frowned.

Sure enough, the black car pulled into the orphanage and parked among several cars already in the parking lot.

"Excuse me," said Derry. She got up and strode across the grass toward the parking lot, leaving me alone on the bench.

I sat bewildered a bit watching her hurry away.

From a distance, I saw her march directly up to the black car and give the just opening door a hasty shove, shutting it on the surprised driver.

The door stayed shut and the window rolled down.

Derry was now several steps back facing the open car window in a angry posture. Her hands were on her hips. She was shaking her head as she talked to someone inside. The door cracked open, but Derry again pushed it shut.

She was not letting out whoever was in the car.

I could tell she just physically wasn't going to allow it. It was way past words. I could hear raised voices, but not make out what the squabble was over.

People in battle are interesting to watch. I decided to step over to see what was going on.

Besides I'm not one who wants to be left out of the violence.

Chapter 40

"I signed your damned papers. It's final. So that's it!" spit Derry.

49

I heard a muffled reply about visitation rights from within the car as I approached.

"Not," said Derry.

"I'll go to court," said the male face in the driver's side window. He had short red hair, a squat face, and rough look as he pointed a finger like a pistol at Derry. His eyes were haggard, his face drained and angry.

"Not till I'm *in jail*," said Derry. Derry looked quickly aside at me as I casually walked within hearing range.

"Just get out of here," she said with a shake of her head at the driver, "There's nothing here for you."

The two faced each other for several long seconds. Then the window rose blurring the face within, and the rumbling black car backed out of the parking lot. It left with a banshee screech of squealing tires as the car turned into the street and sped off.

Derry fixed some invisible hairs at her forehead as she watched the black car disappear, then heaved a great sigh.

I hadn't liked what I'd seen in the face of the driver.

I know all the signs.

Chapter 41

"Sorry you had to see that," said Derry.

"Your husband?" I asked.

Derry nodded, but said, "Let's get out of here, the kids will see me soon and come running. I don't feel like being surround by a lot of needy hearts right now. Can we leave?"

"Sure," I said.

Retreating back into the park, Derry was silent and pensive as we walked. I didn't interrupt her thinking.

"Yeah, that was my husband. Ex now," said Derry to the air before her. "I signed the papers and it became final today. And today's the day he wants to start visitation rights. Can you imagine? Well, never. Never. Never. Never," said Derry. Then her chin quivered and I could see she'd reached the end of holding back her composure.

"It's okay, Derry," I said, "Just let it go."

Derry hunched and cried into her hands. I put my arm around her shoulder.

I was surprised how long we stood there.

Chapter 42

"This has been a surprisingly bad day," Derry said as she gulped in a little air and tried to calm the wracking shivers that held her.

"I'm sorry it's so painful," I said.

Derry nodded thankfully.

"At least I'm glad you're around," she said.

"What a creep," said Derry, exasperated.

"Me?" I joked.

"No, my ex husband."

I could see Derry working back to a stance of anger.

"I grant you're not allowing visitation rights," I said.

"No matter what," confirmed Derry. "No one is seeing my son. Not until this thing is over. I will go to jail. If need be."

"He won't put you in jail," I said.

"Why?" asked Derry bewildered.

"Because if you're in jail, that's all he can do. Then the decision is made, and he can get nothing from you thereafter. If he hasn't gotten your son from you before you go to jail, he can't get him when you're in. You've said you're willing to sit in jail, and if he believes it, then it's not a course of action."

"Maybe so," said Derry.

I could see she'd never really considered going to jail. But now she was.

Derry and I walked slowly back toward her apartment house. I ventured a question or two about her ex-husband.

"You say the trouble with your husband started after the your son was attacked?" I asked.

"Shortly after," said Derry.

"Were you married long?" I asked.

"About six years. About the average life span of a marriage nowadays," said Derry glumly.

52

"Was it a good marriage till then?" I asked.

"I guess, we both worked. I was a bit frazzled running the orphanage and taking care of my family. Jeb was always off on some Real Estate deal. We were kind of like planets each in our own orbit. And occasionally we met and eclipsed. You know."

"But you were surprised when he left you?"

"Very. I guess he met someone better. Some new secretary he took with him on an overseas land seeking venture. I guess maybe it was bound to happen. I can see my part in it."

"How so?" I said.

"Oh, I was wrapped up in the Home and my kids. Giving to my work what should have been given to my family. Maybe that opened the door."

"I don't know," I said with doubt. I couldn't explain what I suspected to her.

"Where does your husband live now?" I asked.

"Oh, he's in our house. It's down by Lincoln, in the Sunset. He's still there, I'm not."

"I did love him, but that's done now," said Derry.

I felt a cold surprise well in my chest, she was speaking so directly to me. For an instant, the pain of potentially losing this person's love became real. She was answering my unconscious questions unasked. And it was me who blinked and tried to hide my fluster.

"Fool," I said.

Chapter 43

We arrived at Derry's flower draped apartment house. It was late afternoon, the 4 o'clock sun was still hot enough to put sweat under your collar. Derry stopped on the building stairs and wrung her hands indecisively. She wasn't sure what was next.

"I want to help you, Derry," I said. "I will, if you'll allow it. I hope you won't try to face all this alone. I know you don't really know me. But you'll have to trust that I can help. I can help," I said.

Derry looked at me a long moment. It was the point of decision of whether she was going to let me, a stranger, into her life.

I hoped my performance had gone well.

"You're willing to help someone who claims she has problems with vampires?"

"You have to admit, it sounds like an interesting problem to solve."

Derry was chewing her lip as she raised an appraising eyebrow at me.

"In truth," I said, "Your vampire problem is *my kind of fun*." I said it with a joshing accent. You can put any accent on the truth you want.

Derry shrugged.

"I don't know," she said, half-convinced.

"There's only one answer for this," I said.

"What's that?" asked Derry intrigued.

"Dinner," I said.

To her credit, Derry laughed.

"So... let me pick you up for a dinner. We can talk some more?"

Though her eyes were doubtful, Derry mustered a nod yes.

Little did she know, but with that nod yes, my grand vampire hunt had begun.

Chapter 44

After setting a time to pick her up, I left Derry and walked back into the park. I walked fairly quickly because I had a lot of ground to cover. As I walked the Eucalyptus landscape toward the ocean, the evening sky was still blue above with a rusty tinge just setting in at the horizon. I walked briskly past park strollers and evening joggers, the tottering aged, and roaming teens. I was headed toward the Sunset.

I came out of the park and walked down Lincoln. In a repeating pattern, I walked South down several blocks on a side street, then cut back to Lincoln again in a zigzag that allowed me to thoroughly look into each driveway and open garage door. I was walking quickly enough that my cane barely tapped the ground, but not so quickly that people sprinkling their ten foot patch of lawn, or single rose bush, would notice.

A person with a cane like me is rather remarkable, but there's no help for it.

Most don't offer a second glance.

After a mile of searching, I found it. The black BMW I'd seen at the orphanage was parked with its sullen black windows drawn up tight in front of a large house. The house was old, with three stories, and a widow's walk around the roof. I imagined the view of the sea was good from up there.

I took a position across the street to inspect the house. It looked a bit like a fortress from the front. It had a high front porch with maybe ten concrete steps up to a solid door. The front was stuccoed a light yellow and the arching fans of two flower trellises stood on each side. The Morning Glory vines on the trellises looked recently dead, a dull and lank gray-green. There was only one window with bars on the ground floor, near the garage door. Large picture windows stood like billboards on the second floor, well above the reach of any burglar's intentions. Beside the house, I could just see the line of a high fence turning like a sentry around to the back.

I saw no sign of Derry's husband in any of the windows. I'd known right away that he was a vampire. A fresh one. And that this was now a little vampire nest. After ten minutes, I hadn't seen him. I was running out of time if I was to get back to pick up Derry for dinner. But I knew one thing.

Where there's one, there's two.

Chapter 45

I went home, had a shower, and changed clothes. I thought about strapping on my orange squirt gun, for a little extra protection, but it would be just too odd if Derry should spot it. Too much explaining to do.

And I had a lot of explaining to do. I was going to have to be convincing to Derry when telling why I knew a thing or two about vampires. Why I knew how to kill them. What I knew and suspected about her son.

The trouble with explaining about monsters is that the story is so far-fetched. It's difficult to get normal people to believe without thinking you're nuts. Derry, of course, was much more open-minded than anyone I had ever met. I imagined it was because she was sharing a bit of the periphery of my world, the dark and isolated realms of hunting vampires.

She was a woman in big trouble. Bigger than even she knew. And I knew a bit about it. And that bit was probably too much for the average human mind.

It's so much easier when you can just walk up and stake a vampire, watch him writhe, gargle in his own juices as he screams, then wrench your trusty cane from his chest to let him fall plop, dead on the rug.

That's easy. That's satisfying.

It's just tougher to explain why later.

Chapter 46

You might ask how I pick out my vampire victims.

Well, it takes one to know one.

The Meeting

Derry's Vampire

Chapter 47

So why? Why, why why.

Chapter 48

I looked across the restaurant table at her.

"You look alarmingly beautiful," I said.

Derry laughed, "Well, that's a straight forward comment."

She wore a black velour dress that took on the shape of her shapely body. At her neck was a little diamond pendant that swung and sparkled in rainbow glitters from a gold-web round her neck. She was immaculately made up. Smiling, she had on dark red lipstick, nearly black, her yellow hair was back in a formal bun, and the thin lines of her eyebrows raised in eagle-wings as she looked at me good-naturedly.

I tilted my head and shrugged.

I like the process of getting to know someone.

And Derry was pleasant company. She leaned over the white tablecloth both arms on the table as she talked. In the background, waiters were walking with hoisted trays of *canard a l'orange* and soufflés, bowing with wines bottles presented on their arms like dueling pistols, or nodding like policemen writing tickets. It was one of my favorite restaurants with plenty of interesting people to watch. The food was also good.

"You look slightly different. I didn't recognize you when you came to the door," said Derry.

I had on a black shirt, black sweater, and dark gray slacks. My cane leaned gently against the next chair.

"I'm in disguise as a human being tonight," I said.

As a vampire, the chance for ironic humor is always tremendous.

I laughed.

Derry wasn't exactly sure why.

"I can't stay out too late, Bill," Derry warned. "Tomorrow's a work day."

"That's what they all say," I said. "I'll take you home whenever you want."

"They all say that, huh?"

"Yes."

"*They all*, would that be dozens?"

"Hundreds, I don't know, maybe more."

"Maybe more?" laughed Derry. She'd raised a shoulder in a gesture of amusement and accusation.

"Maybe none," I admitted. "Since my wife died. None significant anyway."

"I'm sorry. When did this happen?"

"Oh, long ago. Let's not get into it here," I suggested.

"Sure," said Derry.

"None? Since your wife died?" persisted Derry.

I laughed. Then I sobered realizing the answer.

"Well, one."

"And she's no longer around?"

"She's around. But hopefully not around here."

"Her name?"

"Tala. But again let's not get into it."

"Private little muffin, aren't you?" jeered Derry.

"Yes."

"So tell me, if she was here. What would you do?"

"Oh," I said, taking up my walking stick and giving it a cheery little wave. "I'd have to dispatch her with this."

"That's sounds like one way of ending a relationship," said Derry, eyebrows canted at my black humor.

I laughed.

"The best," I said.

Chapter 49

So much of what we know about vampires is balderdash. Most of it foisted on us by Hollywood and the movie industry, which needs ever increasing dramatic effects as opposed to understanding the substance of being. Our inner conflicts are the great conflicts, not the match between Godzilla and King Kong. The great beasts that pull us limb from limb, they are in us. We spend our lives tip-toeing around them, letting sleeping beasts lie. Like me, hoping not to wake up the inner drive for human emotional blood, I work around to focus my attention on vampires.

Take for example the contention that you cannot see a vampire in a mirror. The dramatic effect of that is to provide a hopeful tool for detecting vampires in an effort to stamp them out. If you flash a mirror in someone's face and see nothing, you better grab a stake.

Of course, it's not true. Other people can certainly see vampires reflected in a mirror. I do very much have a reflection. It's just with vampires, driven by their outlaw obsessions, they don't look in mirrors much, and when they do they don't see their own image. They don't recognize it. When I look in the mirror, it's not an empty mirror, but an image of someone else, not myself.

Often I see the face of my intended victim.

However, in general vampires are hard to see. It's because of the truism that vampires can change shape. Very subtly, when we approach humans, we take on the traits our intended is looking for. We project the fatherly concern, the motherly nurturing or reprimand that our intended is secretly seeking for him or herself. Our faces change to show unconsciously recognized family traits, our hair lightens, our smile goes slightly crooked, our laugh becomes so sincere, traits that secretly send the message, I am the one for you. The family traits, unconsciously recognized, that humans respond to. What our victims are looking for, we know how to become. (I've known homosexual vampires who go so far as to put on dresses and wear campy make-up and pasty black eye shadow just to get an interesting victim into an alley. *Mon Chere*, do you like my legs? Oh la la!) We act and project in somewhat cold bloodedness to provide the moment of our victim's recognizing him or herself in ourselves. The victim jumps to the conclusion we share the same longings, the same needs. Then we black-heartedly gobble them up. We feed on those feelings we have raised until there is nothing left.

Then we abandon the husk.

Leaving behind another vampire. Confused, unable to see itself in the mirror.

Soon to start searching its own victims.

At the heart of this you must remember, it is the vampire's occupation to attract others. To make them open up so we can secretly feed. To allay defenses so the most vulnerable human parts may be savored. Licked. Loved. Pulled into our blackness.

If anyone ever says to you, "I could just eat you up!," I think you better watch out.

Chapter 50

Of course, our victims are mainly unconscious of their true desires. So they can't see behind the facade. They can't see us coming.

Chapter 51

Derry began to probe about who I was.

"So do you live in The City, Bill?" asked Derry.

"Yes, I have an apartment not far from the park."

"You'll have to show it to me sometime."

"Sure," I said, meaning never.

"How do you make a living?"

"Well, like I said, I'm retired. So I do what I want. People get lost. I hunt for them."

"How do you make any money doing that?" Derry tilted her head at me to signal interest.

"It's mainly subsistence. I get by." And I'd been getting by for a very long time.

"Were you born in California? Have you lived here long?"

"I was born in France, actually. But moved here long ago."

"You have no accent."

"As I said, it was long ago," I said smiling.

"But your name is Bill? That's pretty American."

"Oh, I'm American. My name is actually Guillaume. Gui for short. Gui Molliere. But that changed to Mauler when I got here. Gui is short for Guillaume, Bill is short for William. Bill Mauler." I shrugged ending the equation.

"And your name?" I asked.

"Derry? Oh, my parents were a combination from the Hippie age. So I guess my mother wanted to call me Delight. And my Dad wanted to call me Fairy."

I raised an eyebrow. Derry laughed in reaction.

"So Derry it is," she said, "they just changed the spelling a little so it wasn't too cowy," Derry bit her lip, stifling a laugh. Then she ended with her own shrug, "It's all I have from them."

"What happened?" I asked. Derry was now picking at her plate looking down.

"I'm not sure really. Some kind of accident in a VW bus. Someone told me dope was involved. I was pulled out of the wreckage, wrapped in a blanket in a cardboard box. That's all they left me. No other papers or identity. Nothing."

"Woa," I said.

"Yes, so I became a mystery child. And wound up in an orphanage at 2."

"And you knew your name?"

"No," said Derry.

"How did you learn it?"

"Oh someone, a hippie, heard about the accident and came down to pick up something of his that was in the VW Bus. The police asked him about me, but he didn't know any last names. Just knew my name was Derry, and how they coined it. He'd only known my parents in passing."

"And the St. George?" I said. "What about your last name?"

"Oh, the orphanage I went to was the St George School for Wayward Children."

"So you chose St. George?" I asked.

"It was better than Derry School or Derry Wayward," she laughed.

"I guess," I concurred.

I looked across at her, a young woman, beautiful in her manners and very feminine in her gestures. Even now she smoothed a leaf of loose hair at her brow with a polished finger tip, a gesture of calm and enjoyment. Her teeth were china white. Her laugh infectious.

Surprising that a lost child could be such a marvel.

Chapter 52

What's it feel like to be a vampire?

Late at night, standing alone in a darkened room, I look out at the moon's bright silver hand-mirror in the sky.

I look out and I feel the vampire calling.

Do you know what it means to look in a mirror and not see yourself? See only your longings and unfulfilled desires? To feel the forever aching call of your empty blood for another?

Perhaps you do.

Perhaps I should get my walking stick and come to call.

Chapter 53

That's why vampires seek victims: to fill the hole in the mirror.

Chapter 54

During dinner, Derry told me of a mistake she'd made once at the orphanage.

"We'd put in a wishing well in the lobby. You know, hoping to collect a few extra donations from prospective parents. Especially those leaving without choosing anyone. Those with slightly guilty consciences."

I looked at Derry and she laughed.

"No, I'm not above that: taking money from the guilty."

"But why was the wishing well a mistake?" I asked.

"We put up a sign: 'Drop a coin, help a dream come true.'"

Derry tilted her head with embarrassment.

"And the kids read the sign and took it to heart. As if it were meant for them."

"A few kids starting dropping in coins. Then more and more."

"Oh, oh," I said.

"And then it became kind of a craze in the Home. Everyone was dropping in coins and discussing wishes. There were arguments over who had the best wish. Who should get theirs first. Who shouldn't get their wish. The price of a good wish caused a lot of fervent policy discussions among the grade schoolers."

"Finally, I had to take the wishing well down," said Derry.

"Why?" All that seems harmless," I said.

"Kids were throwing in whole handfuls of coins like seeds to birds."

"We were making too much money," grimaced Derry. "There'd be several inches of pennies in the bottom of the well each week. Kids were visiting it like the holy grail. Some spent days searching out lost coins on the sidewalk and such. A big game to some, serious work to others. A lot of closed eyes and wishing faces around that well."

"We couldn't let it go on. We had to take the wishing well down. Like a lot of things, we only had it for a brief spell."

"Hope's holiday," I said.

Chapter 55

Of course, there is no wishing well for me.

I am the well.

Chapter 56

"Derry, what's the biggest difference between growing up in an orphanage and growing up in a home?" There had been a short lull in our conversation and I wanted to hear more about Derry's impulse to work with children.

"That's a troubling question for me. Because it really points at what I must work to overcome." Derry put down her fork and sat silent for a moment. Finally, with a resigned smile, she began.

"Most people believe that life in an institution would be pretty grim. Sterile walls. Life in groups. The daily unpleasantness of unbending schedules. But it doesn't have to be that way. In my home for kids, we do our best to provide some spontaneity, to meet individual needs, to provide a sense of fun as opposed to conforming to an organization where children stand quietly in lines in the aisles. "

"But when you ask the real difference, I have to answer this: although I've worked with my employees and staff, tried to teach them about children's needs, tried to point out what their demands really mean — You know, when a kid is screaming because he didn't get a big enough banana at dinner, and his tantrum is demolishing everything in sight, I want my staff to see that what he really means is that he doesn't feel the security and warmth of a parental hug that never came, something he doesn't know about and can't express...Well, I've tried to help my staff see it. See the thing behind children's miseries..."

"But in the end, it comes down to this: my workers, my staff are caretakers. They are the caretakers of many children in our Home. They do their best to do what's right. They work to educate the children, keep the Home in order. They backup the needed discipline within our buildings. But life among caretakers will always be different than in a home."

"Because you can't force anyone to love another?" I said.

Derry nodded and waved her fork in front of her a bit like a conductor calling up the orchestra.

"In the end with my staff, a child that is not your own is one with whom a vital link is missing. A caretaker may wash your clothes, make your food, see to your ABCs. Enlist self-improvement. But something is missing. The children know or sense it. They live among it all their lives with us. Life among caretakers is endlessly disappointing."

Derry grimaced a bit.

"What can you do about that?" I asked. My tone implied the insurmountable.

Derry's chin lifted in defiance.

"I do my best. I do my best to beam it out there."

Then Derry laughed at herself and her choice of words.

"Oddly, the rules are clear. You need be no more than a caretaker. Society decrees we keep these things in careful bounds. One's role in the orphanage is as caretaker, nothing more. Then you've acquitted yourself. You've done the job."

"Children aren't jobs, are they?" I said, with a confirming nod.

"So I think that's the difference, whether you're raised by a caretaker or a real parent. The thing that most affects the direction of children's lives." Derry smiled a half smile.

My mind stretched a bit toward the universal. I said, "I think there are many many more children living under caretakers than we know."

Chapter 57

I looked at Derry, beautiful in herself. I felt old urges I must repress.

I wonder if this isn't the definition of vampire love: this eternal state of desire, unfulfilled longing for another, that by definition is a state of lack, one which most humans quickly trade away for companionship, lack of loneliness. From my point of view, perhaps they should keep and honor that feeling that teaches them the aching human they are.

Chapter 58

We had chit-chatted for about a half-hour at dinner, putting down nearly a bottle of wine to relax us. Derry would occasionally put her fingers to the diamond on her chest like lifting her hand to turn up a dial as she talked. I had asked her more questions about her self, her orphanage and her work, staying away from questions about her husband and family. She seemed rather carefree for the moment.

"So, Bill, why do you want to help me?" asked Derry suddenly.

"I do is all," I said.

"No, 'I do is all' is not an answer," said Derry. "Things aren't as simple as that."

"They aren't." I said.

"So why?"

"I guess I have a profound need to help people in trouble."

"That's kind of a nice airy answer. Seemingly without foundation. Should I believe it?" asked Derry.

"Perhaps not," I said truthfully. She was a bright cookie, as we used to say.

"Why would you want to help people? People like me?" asked Derry.

"Crazy people who think they're pursued by vampires?" I said.

"I guess, if that's what you think."

I cast about in my mind for an answer that was reasonably close to the truth.

"Well, perhaps I was in trouble once, and nobody helped me," I said. "So now, without getting into a long boring story over dinner, I want to help others. I need to."

Derry looked at me gauging my truthfulness.

"Or, perhaps I made a lot of trouble once and now I want to make up for it. Take your pick," I laughed.

"I don't think that last is true. I don't sense you coming at me out of guilt," said Derry. "I sense you're more like a force in pursuit of something. And I'm part of the pursuit, for some reason."

"You're right. Good sensing," I said.

"I'm not here to make atonement for anything. Helping you is something I want to do."

"I think there's more," said Derry.

"Yes, probably," I said.

"But you're not going to tell me right now?"

"No."

"You see, I think it might be a long journey," I added. "We'll have plenty to talk about as we find out about your vampires."

"Well, you're not too communicative a partner here, Bill." Then Derry beamed a smile.

"But at least I've stopped feeling alone."

"Will you tell me the whole story someday?" continued Derry after a pause.

"If we get to know each other well enough," I said.

Derry nodded.

"I think we will."

Chapter 59

And because we vampires are doomed to vampire love, we also inherit its black destructive power. Tremendous power. We can decimate a family, run-over old friends, betray those that trust us most, seed great fields of hurt, humiliation, frustration, woe, abandonment, regret, remorse, irretrievable loss, financial ruin, suicide, even wars (Helen was stolen by the vampire, Paris, who secretly fed for years on Odysseus' raging warrior's blood) ah the list goes on and on. Yes, vampires in their pursuits of vampire love sow great fields of woe, let you harvest it, then burn the whole lot in front of you.

I try to put a cheery face on it, but it's this power that makes me such a God-damned good vampire killer.

Chapter 60

Dinner seemed to be passing by quickly as I enjoyed Derry. She was bright and lively in conversation. She looked for answers behind answers, which kept me on my toes. I had to build her trust, but at the same time give a careful filtering of the truth. You build trust by presenting the truth, yet if the truth was too appalling, you must somehow give it an acceptable face to be known by. Otherwise, your truth is just another stranger in a crowd that others can easily turn their back on.

That, of course, leads to a great sense of isolation, even helplessness.

But I was anything but helpless.

Man, I'm a master slayer. I never forget that. I ought to give myself a little badge that I could wear on the hunt.

The little badge would say, "Let me kill you. It's fun."

Chapter 61

"What do you know about vampires, Derry?"

"Nothing really."

"I looked up some things this afternoon," I said. I sipped my coffee, trying to hide behind my cup.

"What? You just happen to have the Encyclopedia of Dracula at home?" asked Derry.

"A book of myths. Myths often have a kernel of truth disguised in there somewhere, you know?" I said.

"We are talking about my son's life, *you know*?" corrected Derry, "Not some library research."

"Of course, but knowledge may be our best weapon," I said.

"Weapon? That's right, you said you had a military background. So, of course, you'd see it that way."

"And I do," I said.

"What did you learn?"

"If I spoiled the dinner by talking about this, I'm sorry," I said on impulse.

Derry visibly relaxed again.

"That's okay, Bill. I'm just tense about it. Really, let's talk about it, if we must."

"Okay," I said.

Chapter 62

Then I saw him. He made the mistake of looking into my eyes while he was talking animatedly into a wall phone beside the Maitre D's podium. He had a cue ball head with low black crew cut. He was tall, even lanky, in black jeans and a black leather vest exposing bare shoulders and chest, a gold chain on his neck. He was grasping the phone to his cheek as if he were shaving, talking, but secretly looking our way. When he'd caught my eye, he'd suddenly held the receiver out and looked at it as if bitten.

What a dope.

I put him away in the back of my mind, wondering if I could somehow catch up with him later.

In the dark.

"What are you looking at," Derry asked, twisting her neck to see.

"Nothing," I smiled.

"So," I hastened, "Here's the strange thing about your vampire story. As I mentioned, your son didn't die. The vampire did. What if your son has some unique characteristic?"

"You mean, that he can kill vampires?"

"Yes."

"What can that be?"

"I don't know. I've heard you kill vampires with stakes through the heart and such. How much is myth or metaphor, I don't know. And I was thinking about it. A vampire bites a victim and the victim succumbs. They die and are reborn as vampires. If you look at it one way, it's like the passing on of a disease...One vampire infecting another. And so on."

"So?"

"But in this case the old vampire died," I said. "The disease was passed on, it seems, because your son began to weaken, but the diseased host was stopped dead. Something new happened. And it occurred to me something miraculous may have happened."

"I don't see a happy miracle in this at all. What was the miracle you think happened with this vampire my son killed?"

"I think, Derry, you son didn't kill him, he cured him."

Chapter 63

Derry looked at me askance.

I hastened on before her incredulousness could push me away.

"Say some vampires are very very old. They exist by feeding on others, passing on the disease so that they can continue to exist. They go on and on until they are the disease. If you suddenly cure the disease, the vampire dies. There's nothing left."

"And what difference would that be between killing a vampire with a stake?"

"Oh, a big difference. For one you don't always have a stake handy."

I had to make a conscious effort to keep my hand from reaching out reassuringly to my cane. I smiled.

"It also might mean a change in the world. A change in the world of vampires. There would be certain people they would be very afraid of. Certain people they dare not touch."

"Poison candy?" said Derry, her voice low with tension.

"No," I laughed, "The opposite. It's more like people of pure, indomitable blood. People who are their own defense against the vampire realm."

"Just poison candy to vampires," said Derry.

"Well, yup," I said.

Derry swallowed and looked uncertainly around the restaurant. The routine hubbub of people talking over lifted forks, laughing amid the jangle of dropped silverware, ordinary people chewing and looking into their plates, all this must have seemed a distant universe for her, one which she barely belonged to now with the entrance of vampires on the scene.

"And, of course, you can't leave poison candy lying around the house."

"Of course not," I said.

Chapter 64

In an elementary school, I once saw a most interesting Halloween picture of a vampire.

It was a flying stomach with bat wings.

The artistic brilliance was astounding. And I realized this young artist was being approached by a vampire somewhere about.

It took me two weeks to discover it was a crosswalk guard who was secretly offering candy to the kids. Preparing to seduce them.

I ran that son-of -bitch over with a truck.

Then I secretly staked him just before the ambulance arrived.

Chapter 65

"Derry, you are locking your door at night? Right?" I said in testing.

"Of course. I hear you, Bill. I'm taking it seriously."

"Good for you," I said.

"And you're taking it seriously as well. Some people might have just laughed at me. You're not the kind that would come in to take advantage of someone who tells an addle-pated story; you're not the kind who hunts for cripples to abuse, are you?" accused Derry lightheartedly. But it was a testing accusation nonetheless.

"Of course not. I hear you, Derry. I'm not that. I'm in this with you. For my own reasons. But you can trust me on it."

"Like I trusted my husband before he moved on to other interests?" There was a bit of rancor in Derry's voice, mainly aimed at herself.

"Are you lumping me into that wonderfully lumpy category of being a Man? Am I just one in a big bag of rascals?"

Derry smiled at that.

"After the disappointment with my husband, the Number #1 Rascal, I'd rather not meet Rascal #2."

I laughed. "Oh, I'm a rascal all right. But it's more like I'm the Supreme Lord Rascal, avenger of the little rascals and defender of the rascalettes."

"And their pets," finished Derry laughing.

"Oh, I eat their pets if I catch them. I haven't given up all my bad habits," I said.

"You Monster!" cried Derry merrily.

I looked beautiful Derry in the eyes and said as warmly as I could, "That's me."

Derry held my eyes a moment and then blushed.

Then I did as well.

Chapter 66

Most people think that vampires are imbued with tremendous supernatural powers. Hollywood again. Not true actually. Vampires come in all shapes and sizes, powers, and levels of intellect. From the vampire that thought up the mission for the Enola Gay down to that dope in the restaurant. Some of us are supremely powerful and destructive. Others, the most wimpy kinds of vampires, can only make jealousy scratches on the sides of cars.

Chapter 67

I asked Derry if she'd like to go with me somewhere to have a drink before I took her home.

Derry reached out and tilted the white wine bottle on our table to check it. When she let go, it twirled a moment like an ice skater. I knew we were both feeling it.

"Sure, why not." Derry let go a big relaxed sigh." I don't often go to bars. Do you know a place?"

"There's a place I haunt about a block from your place, you'll like it."

"I work tomorrow," cautioned Derry.

"But I don't," I said. "So we'll split the night half and half. First half with me, second half without me."

"Deal."

I called for the check and paid the waiter. I looked around for the cue-ball headed X-generation misfit on the phone, but he wasn't to be seen.

I pulled out Derry's chair and she got up, placing her hand briefly on my arm to catch herself.

"We're a couple of drunken clowns," I whispered.

Derry laughed loud enough that a few heads turned.

"I love spectacles. Especially when they're me," Derry whispered grinning.

And with her beauty and charms, I imagined they often were.

Chapter 68

Richard Nixon was a vampire, a curious one that sustained himself entirely by sucking up everything through the little soda straw of his ego.

Chapter 69

When we got to my car, there was a note on the windshield. I plucked it off and read it before Derry could see.

It said: "Stay away or die. Hierpat."

I knew the cue-ball headed one in the restaurant had written it. Hierpat was slippery. Too cunning. He would never put his name on anything. He was cloaked by a large impenetrable organization. It had to be the dope.

But it gave me a little thrill to think I was on the right track.

I crumpled the note and hid it in my pocket.

The idea that I could be scared off by a note: absurd.

Chapter 70

Ten minutes later, with Derry sitting smiling beside me, asking small questions, I pulled up in front of Big Johns.

Big John's was named after the owner, John the Bartender. Everybody called him John the Bartender, even though he was the owner and the place was called Big John's.

Big John's was a cross between a bar and a rambling coffee-house. There were actually two bushes beside the front door. Inside, your first impression was one of a lot of people, a slouching crowd, lounging at round tables in comfortable chairs, talking and laughing, some in shirt sleeves, shorts, blouses tied shut with knots, sweat pants, and there was even an over -stuffed couch against the wall with couples crushed together side by side tight as books on a shelf. On the far wall was a platform where a quartet of piano, guitar, sax, and flute played rambling jazz over a talking hubbub. It was the kind of place where if someone wanted to sing, they could mount the platform and tell the band to help out.

Big John's had atmosphere. Relaxed, crowded, and human. That much was easily said. It was a place attractive to me. For more reasons than one.

Derry looked around on entering and said, "What a fun place!"

"Let's sit over there," I said and pointed to a secluded table near the wall. People knew me here and I didn't want a lot of interruptions.

Derry and I waded through the crowd, stepping over extended feet in the aisle and asking excusal from people we bumped.

Finally we made it and sat at a table that was slightly damp, just sponged clean.

Sherry the Waitress came up smiling, tray flat against her hip.

"Bill, good to see you. Who's your friend?"

I nodded hello. "This is Derry St. George. Derry, this is Sherry the Waitress."

"You don't have to be so formal, just call me Sherry. Because he doesn't know my last name."

I laughed.

Derry said hello.

"What'll it be tonight?" asked Sherry the Waitress.

"Two more white wines?" I said looking to Derry.

With Derry's nod, Sherry jotted something and said something about a jiffy and left.

"Quite a place!" said Derry loudly.

"Yes, I enjoy it. You can kind of get lost in the crowd and relax here. Watch the circus go by."

"It is kind of a zoo," said Derry scanning the crowd that was talking, laughing, sipping spirits in all shapes and size containers.

Across the room was a long bar with polished top the length of a shuffle board deck lined with gabbing drinkers with their elbows hooked on the bar's edge. John the Bartender was standing behind, a slight sweat on his bald brow. He was a big man in a Hawaiian shirt in blue florals and a white towel over his shoulder.

"That's the owner over there," I said nodding to John the Bartender.

After a few minutes, Sherry the Waitress cruised back to us and placed two goblets of wine on the table.

She left laughing, saying, "I'd a served that to you in coffee cups, like we normally do, but you've got a friend tonight. And we want to impress, right?"

"Thanks so much," I said. I leaned forward gallantly trying to show my appreciation.

Derry was looking at me mouth open.

"Weird," she said.

"This is a good place to watch the human animal," I said. "It's kind of a place where the herd can relax and be itself."

"They don't actually mate here, do they?" smiled Derry.

I laughed. Then it was infectious and Derry laughed, too.

"No, you have to follow them home to their caves to see that," I said.

"Do you find the human animal interesting?" asked Derry.

"Yes, interesting," I said, "And messed up."

"How so?" asked Derry.

"Oh, it seems sometimes, looking around here, that they are so close to happiness. Laughing, talking, enjoying themselves in public, you know. And yet you take them home, and beneath all that is such a mess."

"Such a mess," repeated Derry. "Of course, that's the clinical term."

"Yes. It's in the medical dictionary."

"This human animal, as you put it. Are they worth saving?" asked Derry.

"They seem so close, and yet so far, " I shrugged.

Derry and I now watched a young couple, a smiling boy in clean white T-shirt and jeans, and a girl in a yellow T and jeans cutoffs, both barely into their twenties, stand up and dance beside their table. The young man was handsome smiling and strong. The girl, long black hair swaying down her shoulders, was laughing and leaning against his chest. It was a picture of positives attracting. A healthy laugh through white teeth. A memory of youth and pleasure; an ephemeral as dance.

Such was life at Big Johns.

It was this that I always came to see.

Chapter 71

After a half hour, I sat back, pushing away from the table. Derry and I had been sipping our wine, chatting, and watching the goings on of the bar. I was enjoying Derry's earnest conversation about her orphans. I decided to venture a little of how I saw humans.

"Derry, would you like to hear my theory of human behavior? I call it Bill's Law of Reciprocals."

"Oh yes, do tell," said Derry, amused.

"Is it about you or me?" Derry batted her eyes.

"Both of us, of course," I said. I put my hands to my rib cage like a man about to hitch his suspenders.

"Bill's Law of Reciprocals is this: human behavior is passed down by genes and by behavior. For now, we should mainly be concerned with the behavior part. Agreed?"

"Agreed," said Derry.

"And in my long and ancient history, practically centuries of experience, far outweighing any possessed by you, Derry St. George, Albert Einstein, or any other modern man..."

"Pomposity is charming," broke in Derry.

I nodded encouraged.

"I have come to see this theory of human development. It involves the production of likes and reciprocals in human character."

"I *like* it already," interrupted Derry.

"Of course you do," I laughed, "So now listen, I beg you. Nature's wonder is about to be revealed."

Derry picked up her little black purse beside her and began to rifle through it, saying, "Just a second, I've got to find my tranquilizers..."

I laughed.

"Human behavior is passed on in a funny way. Children inherit a system of values and beliefs. Evolution condones a system of behavior by letting it survive, at least long enough to create new progeny. And I've noted that this passage of human behavior involves the reproduction of likes and reciprocals in human behavior."

"Meaning?" inquired Derry.

"You really want to know?" I asked, "It's a question that may change your life, no turning back."

"So change me, Bubba," said Derry.

"Take, for example, a young girl of five or six, holding her doll tightly to her chest."

"That happens," confirmed Derry.

"Suppose this girl is lonely and her mother can't hold her. Perhaps this girl holds her doll a bit closer to herself. Perhaps she even sings to it."

"That happens," said Derry.

"Well, there you have it!" I said.

"Of course, I totally agree," replied Derry, "What is it that we have again?"

"Bill's Law of Reciprocals! You see, the child is learning behavior. In holding the doll closer to herself, she is comforting herself, even though she is distanced from her true source of comfort, her mother. Like her mother she is distanced from the comforting behavior. But in hugging her doll to comfort herself, she expresses the reciprocal: she learns to comfort her doll, and eventually her own children. She is learning her mothering role. She has learned like and reciprocal behavior at once."

I paused and waved my hand about the busy bar as if I were serving an invisible tray.

"And so it is with all human history," I said with grandeur.

"So, let's see," speculated Derry, "That means you learn two roles at once. And in the scheme of things you'll either turn out like or the reciprocal of your parents?"

"Exact."

"So if your father's a drunk, you'll turn out to be a drunk," prodded Derry skeptically.

"Or an abolitionist preacher," I corrected.

"The spankee becomes the spanker," said Derry.

"Or a person looking to be more spanked."

"Oh, and how does that account for human change?" asked Derry seriously.

"Well, I'm of course speaking of people who unconsciously inherit their behaviors, as, of course, the vast vast majority of human kind always has."

"You see human behavior over time, on the evolutionary scale, is like shouts and echoes. If the behavior is successful in the most basic way—the progeny survive, it repeats itself cyclically. It creates likes or echoing and balancing reciprocals. Otherwise the behaviors die out, the echoes fade across history. It's passed on so perfectly as to be almost unnoticeable, almost magically."

"So you're an unconscious like or reciprocal?" laughed Derry. "What am I?" she dared me to answer.

"Reciprocal," I said calmly.

"And you?" asked Derry without blinking an eye.

"Like," I said.

Chapter 72

I could see Derry was intrigued by my laughable theory.

"And which is better? Reciprocal or like?"

"Well, as you mentioned, in terms of the chance for human change, neither. In extremes of destructive behaviors, you don't want to be like your drunken father. But being the reciprocal is just another form of the same thing. Just as destructive to the human spirit but just in the reciprocal way. An abolitionist preacher's kids may turn out to be drunks."

"Oddly, very oddly, I get a bit of what you're driving at," laughed Derry.

"Wonderful! Nirvana is at hand! Well, maybe something good anyway," I backed off. Ah theater, it's always a temptation.

"So, if you don't want to be like or a reciprocal of what history has handed you, what do you want to be?"

"New," I said.

Chapter 73

"And how do you do that?" laughed Derry.

"Unfortunately, we are old by the time we realize all this. So it is nearly impossible. You must work to make your children new."

"I like that part," said Derry.

"I knew you would."

I could tell by the smile lines under Derry's eyes that she had enjoyed my mocking excursion into the little world of human behavior. She took a small drink of wine now to hide a bit of this enjoyment.

I drank as well.

But to hide other things.

Chapter 74

Here was Derry, beautiful in herself, caring about children, sitting across the table from a vampire. How fair was that? What a great dilemma it posed, her vision of love and change among the children, as opposed to mine. Mine of scouring the earth of my coevals all the time enjoying the pain I wrought. And here I was enlisting her in my quest, as she subtly enlisted me in hers, to save her progeny, to continue her shout and echo on through time.

I think for Derry's shout she would like to hear come back a song.

For my shout, all I could expect to come back was a scream.

Chapter 75

It was then John the Bartender, wiping his hands on his white towel, called across the bar to me.

"Come on, Bill. Give us one," he shouted, nodding his bald head.

A few familiar voices around the bar spoke up in encouragement.

Derry looked quizzically at me.

"What does he want you to do? Sing?" she asked me.

"Recite," I said. I shrugged.

"Recite, poetry?"

"Yeah, I kind of do that as a hobby. Most the bar knows me, and are kind about it."

"Do it," Derry said.

I shrugged, pleading to be let off.

Sherry at the bar called, "Come on, Bill, just one."

Derry stared hard, coaxing me.

"Okay," I said.

I went up on stage and signaled for the band to play. They started with a light flute melody and low bass steps, in beatnik tones and rhythms, as they usually performed for my poems.

I clicked on the mike. I heard a smattering of light applause. Humans are so hungry for anything that speaks to them.

"Thank you, you're kind," I said. "This is a poem for Derry. Whose husband recently left her."

"Sins," I said.

Sins

I'm the kind of man who needs
gobs of forgiveness

for my arrogant chin
for the glassy stare of these merciless sunglasses,
for my hardened insensitivity to others' feelings
as I mumble to myself inside this clam shell

You came to me for understanding, I gave you a joke.
Oh, I'm going to burn for that one.
You came looking for someone to see you, and there I was

standing shaving in the mirror, busy,
holding my nose up in a little pig snout with a mask of clown-
lather on my face

I left you standing on a street corner holding
a big package of your pain
I mailed you little packages of anger always with postage due
Your tears flowed, your heart spoke to the listening ears
of an empty room

As the moon rose through the window like a nightstick of
loneliness

I can't count all my sins against you
I can't count all the stars in the sky
I can't count how many of you there are.

Forgive me,

You came to talk with me,
but I'd forgotten your name,
which is also my own name.

Forgive me my personal and continental slights.
Forgive me for taking off my hands each night
and storing them safely under my bed.
Where was my heart?
Why over there in that little cardboard box the size of a
matchbox   maybe smaller

So, JC, the Lord Up There In Charge of All Forgiveness,
open me up a big account.
So Athena-the-Smiler, Goddess of all Redemption
get out your biggest wheelbarrow to
cart my shit-ridden body on home.
And you, Thor, Dumper of the Great Waters
upon the land, get ready with a big load
to splash down and wash away the sin and shadows
I leave behind on this Earth.

Leave no sign,
Please, clean up after me.

I finished and the band let the music die with a low sax wail. The drinking crowd sat still, looking at me, holding their glasses. I gave a little hand wave as I left the stage.

Then they started applauding and yelling as I sat back down with Derry.

"My God, they love you here," said Derry, leaning over to me as if in a rainstorm. "I'd never guessed you were a poet!"

"It's just one of the things I do, call to people," I said.

Chapter 76

Why would a vampire be a poet, you ask?

I am no longer human, but I sing of humanness to my human companions. So they will know what I have lost.

Chapter 77

Leaving the bar, I walked Derry, merry and a bit tottering, back toward her apartment. As she walked, she took my arm and gabbed and it felt charming and chummy.

"That's marvelous you're a poet," said Derry.

I assumed it was the wine talking.

"Thank you," I said.

"And thank you as well for helping me forget my troubles for a while," Derry drank in the cold San Francisco air with a shrug and sighed.

"I have a secret talent, too," said Derry.

"Oh?" I said.

"Yes," said Derry, "But you won't believe it."

"Try me. I'm looking for things to believe."

"Don't laugh now, but I'm a little bit psychic. I know things ahead of time. And when things are true."

"How so?" I asked. "Tell me more."

As a vampire I should be the last to be skeptical of the paranormal.

"Well, with you for instance, I know you're not telling the truth, about your military intelligence bullshit, but for some reason it's okay."

I nodded without comment.

"I guess this calls for a demonstration," I said finally.

"Okay," Derry laughed, then she looked around.

Ahead of us on the street, under the dim light of street lamps, a man had just exited his car parked at the curb. He wore a long raincoat, unbuttoned, and was searching his pants pocket for something.

"For example," said Derry, "That man's about to fall down."

I watched. The man opened his trunk and pulled a new broom out and set it against the car. The man then bent into the trunk again and retrieved a loaded brown grocery bag.

"Nothing so far," I said.

Then the broom slid from the car and fell on the sidewalk with a slap. The man, wobbling with the grocery bag, stepped forward onto the broom handle which slid like a banana peel. The man dropped on his back on the sidewalk and the paper bag burst spreading groceries all over him.

I looked on amazed.

"See?" giggled Derry.

"How did you know that?" I asked.

"I don't know, I just do," said Derry delighted that I was a bit in awe.

"You sure that man just doesn't get out of the car and fall down every night?" I accused.

Derry laughed. "No, I can tell when some events will happen."

"What about me? What am I thinking?" I asked.

If she mentioned I was a vampire, I was going to run.

"Sorry, I can't read minds or anything. It's just sometimes I sense things will happen."

"How long have you been able to do it?"

"Since I was a kid. But I learned not to do it. It scared people, and then they scared me, acting spooked out."

I imagined so. If I told anyone I was a vampire, first they laughed, then they'd feel very uneasy around me.

"What about the event in the park today? Why didn't you foresee that?"

"I was very disturbed, worrying. Worrying about another feeling I'd picked up. Then maybe I did actually know..."

"What do you mean?"

"I have a feeling something terrible will happen soon. Maybe I just wanted to get it over with."

I looked at Derry trying to comprehend.

"You see, like most unusual talents," continued Derry, "My psychic thing is also a great burden."

"A burden in what way? It seems you should go to the racetrack everyday," I said.

Derry drew in a long draught of cold air into her lungs.

"Because, Bill, I have a sense I'm going to lose somebody close to me soon, and there's nothing I can do about it."

"Are you sure?" I asked.

"Oh yes. And I'm very worried. I'm worried about the vampires. I think they're coming back."

"And you're worried you'll lose someone to them?"

"Yes."

"Can you intervene when you know these things will happen?" I asked.

Derry shrugged, not knowing the answer.

Derry clasped my arm and pulled me closer to her smiling, "Enough of this and my troubles. Let's just walk me on home, Bill. I feel safe with you."

I nodded.

"Derry," I said, "There's just one thing I want to know."

"What's that?"

"Do you see me flopping down on the sidewalk in the near future?"

Derry laughed. "Not in the next six or seven minutes or so. So you're probably safe till I get home."

We walked and chatted as we headed back to her apartment. But in the back of my mind I kept thinking how she expected to lose someone close to her soon.

As we walked my cane tapped an unsteady rhythm on the cement.

Chapter 78

Arriving at her door she pulled out her key and turned to thank me.

It was the typical opportunity to kiss her, but it was too soon and I held back.

"Thank you, Bill, for everything."

I looked at her.

"I'd like to help you, Derry," I said.

"I know." She made no further explanation.

Derry invited me in for coffee.

I had been sitting on the couch for several minutes when Derry brought in a tray with several cups, a coffee pot, and a small plate of brown objects that I took to be cookies.

Derry smiled at me, her blond pony-tail wagging, as she poured my coffee then looked over to see if I took sugar. I nodded.

"So, Bill, you were married?" she asked.

"I was once," I said. I picked up my coffee cup and sipped from it, hiding behind it like an impossibly small shield. But Derry didn't let me off.

"Do you have children?"

"I did, a daughter, but she died."

"How so?"

"Oh, it's a long story, one that happened long ago. I'll tell you someday. I have no one in my life right now."

"Except me," joshed Derry.

"Yes, Ms. Psychic Powers of 1998."

"Recite another of your poems for me, will you?" asked Derry.

I turned a bit red about the ears. That's highly unusual for a vampire, to experience any kind of being flustered.

I grimaced and shook my head no.

"Come on," said Derry. "I've never had anyone recite a poem just to me."

"Okay," I said, relenting. I am enough of a showman to step up on the stage.

"This one is called 'As I was'." I took a breath and began. It was a poem about me before I became a vampire.

As I Was

Though the clouds are near today
you can touch them with your hand,
the ocean is distant and white capped

like me

How can I tell you I love you when I can't even tell that to myself?

Loneliness rolls up into the floating smoke-ring of addictions.

I don't know how to say these things to you.

If I was to have an Indian name it would be Little Oaf,
or Turtle Who Loves Stones, or
 Man Who Carries Snow In A Bucket Instead Of His Heart

"That's a sad one," Derry said after a few seconds of silence.

I nodded. "Is it too gross for someone to indulge themselves like that?"

Derry shook her head.

"It must be wonderful to express your feelings in poetry."

"I don't really express my feelings," I said, "It's more like I describe the feelings I once had. My memory of them."

Derry looked at me strangely.

"I also write when I have something to say to humans," I hastened on.

"Humans?" said Derry, perking up at hearing an odd expression.

I smiled, covering up, "as opposed to *vampires*."

"Do you think we live in a world that has both, or are you just humoring me?"

"Both, " I said in sad admission. I knew this to be utterly true.

We sat in silence for nearly a minute, I looking into my black coffee for protection, Derry putting a few extra lumps of sugar in her own. I glanced over at her and saw her wonderful angelic profile. Her eyebrows were slightly arched as she smiled at something she was thinking.

"So, Bill, what were you telling me with that poem?" Derry looked at me with mischievous challenge.

"Be careful, Derry," I said.

"For a woman supposedly surrounded by vampires, I guess that's good advice," said Derry. Then she added, "However lame-ass it seems."

I laughed.

"Would you like to visit the orphanage with me tomorrow where I work?" asked Derry.

"Yes," I said.

"I know," said Derry. Then she laughed with her psychic powers at work.

We set up for me to swing by and pick her up at 9:00 o'clock the next day.

Chapter 79

I didn't tell Derry that in my mind humans were barely-civilized animals. Albeit they had their laws and straight lines, they could barely live between them.

And under the bright and shiny moon,

I was just a plain wild animal.

Chapter 80

My foot had just touched the top stair when I saw a shadow recede off my car.

I gripped my cane and jumped the remaining steps into the street. When I hit the sidewalk, it was empty, so I sprinted left into the alley leading behind Derry's building. My cane was at port arms so I wouldn't bang or snag it against the objects I charged past.

I run pretty quietly. But you have to watch out not to startle prowling cats that panic and throw themselves noisily into the sides of garbage cans and off fences, screaming and clanging into whatever, as they escape. This tends to alert the prey.

The alley was clear to the end of building, but I knew he couldn't be far ahead.

I tagged the building corner and stopped to look around.

Sure enough, there he was, the imbecile, slowing to a walk. He'd just passed a great blue-black dumpster, shoulder high, and was stepping behind it to peer back down the alley. The light was dim, a full moon just breaking the horizon, hulking shadows of cars and garbage cans pooling on the concrete.

Since I knew where he was I stepped out into view.

I began walking determinedly down the lane and his head jerked back behind the dumpster as he took cover.

I set my pace and intentions to say I was hurrying to the end of the alley still a half-block away.

The fool stayed planted thinking I was going to walk right by.

But as my shoulder cut the edge of the dumpster, I swung my cane, pointing it into the black grotto beside the dumpster where I knew he was crouching.

His mouth opened, startled to find the cane's silver tip aimed at his belly. His eyes darted left and right, thinking to escape.

"Get up!" I said gruffly.

I reached out and jerked him by the chest into the alley. I pushed him up against the dumpster. Then I put the tip of my cane to his chest.

"Stand still," I said.

He nodded and swallowed at that.

I reached into my pocket and shook out the crumpled note that I'd found on my windshield at Big John's.

"Did you write this?"

Pressing his back against the steel frame of the dumpster, I could see he was reviewing his options. Which weren't many. I could see he believed I just might kill him. Sweat shown on his cue-ball brow.

"Tell, you wrote it. This is not from Hierpat, right?"

"I wrote it, so what, Brother. You should mind it." His voice was a bit raspy.

"Have you seen him tonight or did you just write this yourself?"

Something about this made my captive smile crookedly. "You're dying to know," he said straightening, lifting his chin a bit haughtily.

"No," I said, giving the cane a nudge to make it bite his chest, "You're dying to know."

I began to apply steady pressure to the cane, pushing it with two arms into his sternum.

He blinked, his mouth open.

I'd made an impression.

"No, I wrote it, I wrote it, don't!"

"I'm happy to hear that," I said.

"Listen, I want you to give this message to Hierpat the next time you see him," I said.

That single sentence must have told him he was nearly safe. The look of arrogance that flooded his face! You'd have thought he was going to spit on me. Ah, vampires! Amazing resilience in the depths of ignominy.

"Tell him this," I said, "Welcome to Hell."

I rammed the cane completely through him, the tip clanking behind into the dumpster's steel.

He only wiggled and shuddered a bit. Just a little drool.

Ah, but the surprised look on his face! Joy! Ecstasy to behold!

Chapter 81

When I pulled the cane free, I stood thinking a minute. No one, no dogs barking, still silence in the alley. Only one light on high in Derry's apartment balcony. And as I looked up, the light went off. I grabbed and dragged him by his leather vest down the alley to another apartment building dumpster. I hefted him up and into it, then quietly closed the lid.

Garbage disposal is one of society's most important functions.

Chapter 82

As I walked home, refreshed and exhilarated by my little exertion, high in the sky flew a great yellow full moon.

Humans were such complex animals, but the big things like the moon were so simple...

I have always loved looking at a brilliant moon.

It makes me feel such a lovely empty.

Chapter 83

The weirdest vampire aberration I've ever heard was a vampire couple who worked as a team.

They staged midnight car breakdowns on dark roads.

Mrs. Vampire, a comely female, would stand beside the car. Mr. Vampire waited away in the bushes.

If an honest driver stopped and offered help, Mrs. Vampire thanked him and waved him on.

But some time during the night the rapist would arrive.

The rapist gets out of his car, approaches Mrs. Vampire, attacks and drags her into the bushes. There is Mr. Vampire. He puts a gun to the rapists head and says, "What are you doing to my wife?"

He throws the rapist on the ground. He holds up a cut broom handle. He says, "We have a little surprise for you tonight. You're going to find out what it's like to be raped."

Sure enough, they pull down his pants and Mrs. Vampire rapes him.

They leave him there half-naked to think about it with a stick up his ass.

And then they drive off bellies full of laughter.

Chapter 84

I looked at Derry as her apartment door opened.

"What's wrong?" I said.

Ashen faced, she had only opened the door halfway.

"It's not a good day for me to take you to the orphanage," said Derry swallowing her words.

"What's happened? Has something happened?"

"No, I just can't take you. Another time. Perhaps."

Derry went to close the door.

I put out my cane and stopped the door from shutting. Derry violently winced.

"Derry, what's wrong?" I began to push into the room.

Finding she couldn't hold me back, she relented and backed away.

Her face was stony and closed as she cast wary glances at me.

I ventured one step into the apartment.

"Tell me, Derry," I coaxed. "If something happens, and we're to work on this vampire business together, I've got to know. We have to trust in each other."

Derry's mouth pursed.

"Tell me," I said. "Did something happen last night, after I left?"

Derry looked at me.

"Yes," she said. It sounded like an insult.

"What was it?"

Derry raised her chin and looked hard at me.

"Last night, I saw something in the alley."

I blinked.

"It was dark. I looked out on the alley from my balcony. The moon was just coming up. I saw two men. They seemed to be fighting or something."

"What happened?" I asked guardedly.

"I couldn't see them clearly. It was dark."

"And?" I asked.

Derry squared her shoulders and looked at me, eyes underlined with fear and distrust.

"And...I saw one of them push his cane through the chest of the other."

Then Derry's eyes were like those of an enraged falcon.

I had to admire her courage.

Chapter 85

Disaster.

I knew now all my careful plans for managing our relationship were out the window.

Chapter 86

"Please leave. I need to go to work." Derry raised a leading hand toward the door.

I pushed the door shut behind me and locked it.

Then Derry looked truly frightened as she backed across the room.

I went over to the sofa and sat down with my hands folded in my lap.

"Derry, it's okay to be afraid," I said.

I could see Derry, undecided, standing there tense with the shallow breathing of an animal about to flee.

"You know I'm not here to harm you. You know it, don't you?"

I interlaced my fingers and shrugged.

"Derry," I started, "What you saw was correct. It was me in the alley. I killed that man last night. I'm sorry, I can see you're terrorized right now. I don't know how to handle this other than the truth. So brace yourself. I killed that other man...because he was a vampire."

Derry was blinking dazed a bit with this confession.

"Don't refuse to hear me out, please."

"There're...too many questions. I..." Derry stammered.

"Sit down if you wish. Let me tell you—"

"No, I won't sit."

"Fine," I said. I drew a breath wondering where to begin. Explanations are generally not my style. Not many are generally left hanging around to make explanations to.

"I killed him because he was a vampire, Derry. I killed him because it's what I do. I'm a vampire killer."

"How could you do that! I saw you! It was so gruesome."

"It's the only end a vampire can meet."

"You're a vampire killer? What does than mean?" asked Derry.

113

"Remember I said I was a hunter? Well, I am. It's just that I hunt an animal that is making you its prey. Vampires."

"What? How did you become that?"

"It's kind of a long story on how one becomes a vampire killer. I will tell you, if you want to hear it someday. I will. It's a not too pretty calling. Gruesome as you say. But I heard of you and came to you because you need me. You have vampire troubles, which I can help solve."

"You're not anything that I thought you were!"

"No, Derry," I said solemnly. Derry was like a blind person locked in a black room trying to feel her way out. And she'd just discovered a monster (me) was in there with her.

"You killed that man."

"Not man, that vampire."

"How do you know he was a vampire?"

"It's hard for me to tell you. There's no satisfactory answer. You know, Derry, it's like your psychic ability. If you told people, it spooked them out."

"Are you telling me you have vampire ESP?" asked Derry.

I shook my head solemnly.

"Well, give me the unsatisfactory answer then. I don't know you. You could be a vampire yourself for all I know."

I made a pained half smile.

"Derry, I am."

Chapter 87

Derry's diaphragm convulsed and her hand raised to her mouth as if to catch her gasp.

I realized it was unlikely Derry would be accepting my invitation to the *Vampire Cotillion*.

Chapter 88

It may have only been a moment, but it seemed there was an eternal silence between us.

Too much had been exposed. Derry was dazed and confused. I had no plan and there was no filter for the truth I could put on it.

We were at the impasse of two opposites meeting. Derry might scream and run out the door, grab a fireplace poker and come at me, or wilt and give up. I didn't have a clue.

Usually my vampire powers of disguise never failed me. My wit played through. My charm and seductiveness cut away the protective clothing to expose quivering flesh and desire. Not here.

I was a vampire standing naked before a human. Not the other way around.

"There are things you need to know," I said.

Derry looked at me her face blank.

All I could think of was to show her the lightening path.

"Derry, you know you have vampire problems. I'm a vampire. And a vampire killer. You must accept me if you are to solve your problems."

To me, this was tantamount to telling someone trapped in a cave without light, panicked, to go deeper into the blackness.

But it was true. It was her only hope.

She had to be alone with me, the monster, in this terrible unyielding darkness.

"Call up all your abilities, Derry, and know what you need to know," I coaxed.

Eternity stretches so long. And it comes at you everyday.

Finally she nodded.

Chapter 89

Then something strange happened. I felt my own tears almost brim to my eyes. Here was someone who wanted to know me. I blinked them back and smiled bitterly.

Impossible. That's out of range of vampire behavior. Yet this extraordinary woman was going to listen. Listen to the revelation of my entire being, in all its sordid power, before her.

Because she needed me.

Ah, the ironies of life.

I saw the smallest flame of curiosity light Derry's face as she saw me struggling with myself.

She saw she wasn't the only one that was nearly out of control.

"Where do we begin?" Derry said calmly.

I raised my hand to the couch.

"Let's talk."

Chapter 90

"So much of what you said was a charade," said Derry.

"The charade is over."

"And I was right, none of your retired military story was true."

"No, not much."

Derry took a shallow breath before beginning her questions in earnest.

"But my vampire problem is true. Because you're admittedly a..."

"Yes," I said.

117

"I don't feel you're going to harm me. But you are out to harm others."

"Yes."

"Are you after my son?"

"No."

"Why not, if other vampires are? There are other vampires after him, right? You've said that. And you must know."

"Yes, there are other vampires after him. One in particular that I want to meet up with."

"So why don't you want to harm my son?"

"I'm a very rare breed of vampire, I guess. I'm a vampire killer."

"Do you harm...humans? People like myself, I mean?"

"Once...before I began my present...pursuit."

"Which is killing people in alleys with your cane?"

"There are other ways as well, which I'll tell you of."

"If vampires sustain themselves by feeding off others, why? Why don't you? Why aren't you after my son?"

A key question for Derry.

"I sustain myself by feeding off the blood of my dying brethren."

"You drink vampire blood?" exclaimed Derry with a grimace.

"No, there is no such thing," I laughed. "Simply killing them does the trick."

Chapter 91

Derry questioned me for over an hour. She sat on a couch by the fireplace, her hands between her knees, shoulders hunched as if very cold.

I was sitting six or seven feet away, keenly aware of the distance between us.

I'd explained that there were many types of vampires in the world. Another invisible world that went on daily around us.

"And they don't all work as individuals. Some are organized. I like to think of them as working in packs. But it's not exactly true. There is a large underworld organization, managed hierarchically. With leaders, and group captains, and even human henchmen."

"Armies?" asked Derry.

"Armies out for blood, anything they can get," I said.

Derry shuddered visibly. Her problem was growing by the minute.

"And these organized vampires, they're after my son."

"I believe the leader is. A particular vampire that I'm very interested in meeting up with."

"Meaning doing your cane thing?" asked Derry.

"Yes, doing my thing," I confirmed.

"His name is Hierpat."

Chapter 92

"Why do you need *me* to go after this Hierpat?"

"Being a vampire killer, I'm not exactly privy to their world."

"Why don't they just kill you?" asked Derry.

Of course some had tried.

"They don't really know much about me," I said.

"Why is that?"

"None of Hierpat's underlings who has ever met me has reported back."

A silence set in between us.

Derry squirmed uncomfortably.

"You're that good?" asked Derry.

"I'm that good."

Chapter 93

"So this Hierpat and his clan, they don't know anything about you?"

"They only have a sense of me, from the missing ones that never turn up. For them, it's like the void that indicates a black star. They haven't seen it, but I imagine they sense it's there."

"But why do you need me to find this Hierpat?"

"Vampire life is very ethereal, shadowy, it's hard to penetrate. He's protected as well by his surrounding organization."

"How long has this been going on?"

"Vampires? Since the beginning of human time."

"And you, how long have you been a vampire killer?" asked Derry.

"Too long," I shrugged.

Chapter 94

There was a very long silence between us.

Then she said it. Said it to the air before her.

"You're using my son as bait."

Chapter 95

There was no reply to that. For me to track down Hierpat, it was necessary to know where he was going. What he was after. This was a nearly impossible task. Like one fish free among a thousand in a large pond, he could go anywhere, go after anything he wanted, and always be nearly invisible among the many.

If I could poison the whole pond, I would. But there wasn't enough poison in the world. There wasn't enough time to squirt every nasty vampire I saw in the face. Hunting and skewering took so much time. Ah me, the never ending housework of a vampire killer. All my deadly little chores to do each night culling the vampire world.

Meanwhile Derry sat looking at me incensed, her eyes piercing blue, her mouth a hyphen connected directly to her disapproval.

Using her son as bait.

Yes.

But not for food.

Chapter 96

"You'll never see him. You'll never find him. I won't take you to him. Ever," stated Derry with finality.

I nodded.

"If you can do your vampire thing that way, fine. But I will not let you near him," Derry persisted.

I nodded again.

"Agreed," I said reassuringly.

I knew, and Derry perhaps knew, that this was not true. You cannot protect someone by not knowing where they are, by not being near. And unspokenly, Derry was going to let me be near her, and thus near her son.

"Agreed," I said again.

Chapter 97

Derry began to probe a bit into what I was going to do.

"And, so, what happens now?" she asked.

"I watch. I must be around, get to know your world a bit. I watch. If you can help me, that is better. But you need me to meet them, to stop them. This is the way left you."

"So, it's fight fire with fire."

"No, fight ice with ice."

I'm quite the quipster.

Abruptly Derry shook her head and tears fell clear from her face. Overwhelmed, she shuddered. Then she set her jaw and quickly took a deep breath to control herself. She glanced hard my way, first to make sure I hadn't advanced on her, second to send a message to check me if I meant to.

"We are an amazing costume party, huh, Derry?" I said, "I'm so sorry for my part, for the sudden revelations of the horrors beneath. I can see it's almost more than you can bear. I can see it."

"And although it's just me, you're not alone."

Derry nodded as if to herself.

As vampire, I'm used to living through things that would break the average person's heart. I'm used to it.

I just don't like it.

Chapter 98

Derry's phone rang. She startled, then looked left to the black instrument calling from the table.

After a glance my way she got up and went over to it. She lifted the receiver to her ear.

"Hello?"

A short pause.

"Hello? Hello?" asked Derry quizzically.

She looked at the receiver then set it back in its cradle.

"No answer. Wrong number, I guess," said Derry returning to her spot on the couch.

I wondered if a little boy's voice had answered the phone whether Derry might have had unexpected visitors soon.

Chapter 99

After the interruption by the phone, Derry's daily life seemed to surface and she looked at her watch.

"I must go to the Home," she said.

"Take me with you," I said.

"No!"

"Derry, please. I'd enjoy seeing your workplace. It's a good idea."

"I'm not taking a..." Derry's voice trailed off.

"Vampire," I finished.

"A vampire into my place of work. No way."

"I don't mean to affront you. I realize all this is too much to accept by most anyone. The blackness I bring into your life, I know it's great weight and burden. But Derry, I must be where you are. I am a part. I will go to your orphanage no matter what you say. It's just better if you invite me."

I could see Derry realize that if I was guarding her, she also had to guard me.

"We're stuck with each other."

"So be it," Derry said stoutly.

That brought a smile to my lips.

Chapter 100

Derry looked at me sternly.

"There's just one thing I want to know. How did you find me? What brought you homing in on me and my family?"

"One of Hierpat's little helpers told me," I said.

"Why would one of Hierpat's men—"

"Vampires," I interrupted.

"Vampires," said Derry taking in my correction with a slight condescending nod, "tell you about me?"

"Because he was begging for his life," I said.

Derry stepped back from me. She was comprehending what I was. She was getting a glimmer of what it is to be a vampire-killer.

I raised my chin. Let her see me in my black and horrid glory.

Finally I relented and looked at the ceiling saying, "Derry, it's ugly, and it's what I do. It's what I do. It's all I can do. As a vampire, I can do nothing else."

It was Derry's turn to look at me. Her face registered eminent repulsion, then changed to something else.

"I'm so sorry," said Derry.

Chapter 101

Derry stood like a sentry beside the door holding it open for me. I stepped into the orphanage and came face to face with a huge bouquet, a wild spray of chrysanthemums, purple gladiolas, daisies, orchids, even weird orange bird's of paradise heads up like storks, in a multicolored passle standing at attention on a polished table.

As Derry brushed past me, she noticed I'd stopped at the flowers.

"The local florist, just down the block, Lord's, he loves kids..." said Derry.

"The Lord loves kids because he always makes them new, " I said.

Derry hesitated, gave me an appraising look.

Just then a red hair woman bustled up and nearly attached herself to Derry's elbow.

"'Morning, Derry. I need your signature on these purchase orders, so we can take delivery this afternoon. And this bottom invoice is Drotmyer's, that old fool's double-billed us again."

"I'll call him this afternoon." As she signed, Derry inclined her head toward me saying, "This is Bill Mauler, he's here to visit. Bill, this is Henrietta Smit, our bookkeeper."

"And know it all," said Henrietta. She smiled at me, waved the sheaf of papers, then trotted off across the lobby toward a wooden door.

"This way," said Derry.

We crossed the lobby, which was wide and open, with a large Rabati rug in its center. Couches, end tables, and even magazines were stationed conveniently here and there. Large wooden beams hung high overhead. In general the place had the feel of a large hunting lodge or resort, except with small touches that made it a lot more welcoming.

Kids were stationed here and there. Some sitting together, poking and leaning on each other on a couch. Others squatting in corners intent on their playing hands. Others I only saw briefly as they entered and chased each other out again. There were intermittent squawks and giggling. A few were walking carrying books or peegees. They were decently dressed, but nothing exotic. No red or green hair, or nose rings. Most too young for that.

Several immediately came up and surrounded Derry in a smiling circle. She looked down on them pleasantly, hearing the morning's complaints and kid hellos. I watched her as she patted backs, squeezed shoulders, and touched cheeks, listening and giving encouraging comments that granted the children the ability to nod and leave her. For a while there were seven or eight around her waist, then moments later, they were leaving.

"I do quite a bit of mothering," said Derry.

"If we could bottle it, you'd make a lot of money," I said.

We walked up to long mahogany desk where a gray-haired woman sat like a receptionist at a hotel.

"Hi Hilda, what's the report?" asked Derry.

The gray-haired woman looked up and smiled. "Two in the infirmary, but just colds and fever. One breach. You can speak to him this evening."

128

"A breach?" I asked.

Derry looked at me and smiled, "A breach just means we had someone stay out last night too late. Missed the curfew. We have teenagers who occasionally roam at night. Just to get out of here. We call it a breach of faith."

"Not like a breach in security," I said.

"No, of course not. Just a small infraction. Occasionally adventure calls one of our teens, boys and girls, out at night. I talk to them about it."

"That's not good, going out at night late, especially teenagers."

"Can you name one that hasn't done it?"

I smiled and shrugged.

"This is Hilda Johnson. Hilda, this is Bill Mauler, a visitor today."

Hilda granted me a cordial nodded.

"Are you looking to start a family?" asked Hilda.

"No," I laughed, "Thanks anyway."

Derry looked at me impassively.

"Just trying," said Hilda magnanimously. "I'm good at my job, aren't I, Derry?"

"Oh yes," said Derry. "Just be sure to check the parent's rap sheets for murder before we sell them one."

Hilda laughed and nodded. But Derry gave me a cool look.

A blond-haired boy, a cherub-faced five-year-old ran up to Derry and threw his arms around her knees. Derry stiffened, then bent and hugged him back.

"I have things to tell you," said the boy, smiling up.

"Good! Mrs. St. George will come to see you in a while!'

"Who's that?" asked the boy.

"Just a man come to see the Home," said Derry. "Now you hurry off, I'll see you later..."

"Cool cane! Can I see it?" asked the boy.

I held it out to him. "What's your name?"

"Kelly!" The boy stepped forwarded eagerly for the cane, but Derry intervened.

"Kelly, let's leave Mr. Mauler's cane alone. He might not want people playing with it." Derry's hand was pressing on the boy's chest backing him up.

"Who knows where it's been," said Derry directly to me.

Kelly made a disappointed face and backed away to leave.

"I'll see you later, okay?" called Derry to the retreating boy.

"Who knows where it's been?" I said to Derry. I realized Derry must think my lovely cane was something I stirred garbage with.

Funny, I can only think of it as immaculate and beautiful.

Chapter 102

We walked down a large hallway as Derry gave me a tour. On one side of the hall were several large classrooms with immense curtainless windows. Filling the room, hulking blond Formica topped tables stood with an audience of empty chairs hugging their rims.

"Do the kids attend class here?" I asked.

"No, they go to the public schools in the area. Those rooms are mainly for after school work, study halls. It's pretty noisy sometimes in the dorm rooms upstairs."

As we walked, passing kids called cheerful hellos to Mrs. St. George. With each greeting Derry's face lit and she nodded back with great warmth. Funny, but this recognition alone seemed to give the children something, brighten them as they passed.

"I have a meeting with prospective parents in about 15 minutes. I'd like you to stay near my office till I come back." Derry's look was stern contrasted to the greetings she'd just given her charges.

"No problem," I said.

There was something free and lively about the hallways I liked. It was well lit, and a bit expansive, enough perhaps to tempt young hearts to run. In deed, I saw two boys, second or third graders, skid into view in tilted Charley Chaplin slides as they rounded a corner, one chasing the other with a raised book for a quick whack. They saw Derry and I and slid to a halt.

"Enough of that! Stop or I call the Hilda who will dismantle your both and store your parts in the basement for kids who need them!" Derry shouted this with patently false anger.

The boys nodded and began to walk, at least until they disappeared around the corner. Then I heard a slap and running feet once more.

"At least they're self-punishing," I said.

Derry sniffed good naturedly.

"My office is this way," said Derry.

I noticed she was walking more relaxed next to me now.

Then we passed a black doorway. I glanced in to see a large room, filled with sofas squatting at odd defensive angles to the door, and the pale blue face of a TV high on a wall. There didn't appear to be any windows, or at least they must have been covered, for the interior was so dark that it was difficult to see the occupants. Grey ghosts were playing across the face of the TV. As I looked into this TV room, I had the sense that the floor was littered, but couldn't really tell by what.

"That's our Lair of Despair," said Derry. She grimaced.

"What?" I said.

"It's where the kids who can't really handle it tend to retreat. You know, the kind who wear black T shirts, black makeup, black hair, black everything. And they kind of sit passively, cynical, with nothing to do. And often they passively get into a lot of trouble."

"How so?"

"Oh, they kind of go along with drugs and drinking. They hang out with the homeless and despondent. Trouble finds them."

"It is a black room," I said. A grand nursery for potential vampires.

"And a full-time job trying to pull kids out of there."

"I imagine," I said.

"Can you?" asked Derry in half-accusation. "People prey on them..."

Derry looked her meaning at me.

132

"Yes, I know," I said.

Chapter 103

We came to a door in the hallway with a bench beside it. The door looked to lead into a classroom with no intervening reception area. On the door was lettered the word Director.

"I work here. My meeting is soon," said Derry. "Would you mind waiting here? It'll be probably about a half hour."

"No problem,"

"Please stay here," said Derry with some gruffness.

Just then Hilda appeared at the far end of the hallway walking an impassive-faced couple into view. They were in their forties, a bit ashen, as if they were treading on unfamiliar ground and might think to escape. But something about the way the woman clenched her purse to her stomach made me think she was leading the way. Both were dressed as if going to church, with crisp shirts, cuffs, polished shoes, dark coats and starched smiles. I realized this may seem like some kind of audition to them.

Hilda waved cheerily and called, "We're here!"

Derry called, "This way, good to see you!"

Stepping up to bat, the man reached out and shook my hand, "John Moyer, Mr. St. George. Glad to be here."

I looked sideways to Derry.

Derry stepped forward with her hand out to repair the damage, "Glad to meet you, John, my name is Derry St. George, the Director here."

John's wife looked quickly at him with reproof and his cheeks reddened slightly.

"No harm, people mistake me for a real person all the time," I said.

"Pay no attention to the man behind the curtain," broke in Derry, "He's a complete idiot and doesn't belong here!" Derry smiled warmly, but gave me a bit of evil eye.

John came to and introduced his wife, who shook Derry's hand but not mine.

"This way," invited Derry, opening her door, "I'll explain the adoption process, and then answer any questions or concerns."

"You, wait there for me," said Derry to the bench as she closed the door.

Then I was alone with Hilda.

"Can I get you some coffee or something?" Hilda asked.

I sat, shaking my head no.

"Well, I'll just leave you then," and the busy Hilda went bustling down the hallway from the direction she came.

I decided to watch the passing orphanage traffic for a while.

Chapter 104

Funny thing about vampire life, no matter where you are, it isn't boring. There's always someone, something, potential victim or not, stirring about. Go to the movies, you can watch the movie or the people. Get on a bus, watch your fellow passengers or watch the passing cars move like trays in a cafeteria. Roaring vampires live in a world of appetizers and hors d'oeuvres. Watch a boxing match and decide if you'd like to consume the victor or the slain. Watch a football match and wonder if you could consume them all.

It's a full and bountiful world.

But, of course, after the surfeit, you realize there isn't much joy in it.

It's something like venturing to a new restaurant to try a little *steak au cheval* and finding the waiter leading out a horse.

Some vampire tastes run from savoring the rudest flavors to those of the highest delicacies. Like in the olden days, some might get hooked on blacksmiths. Others fencers. Ballerinas. Eunuchs. Clowns. The pristine innocence and vulnerability of the retarded. Still others choirboys, a predilection that still exists today.

Amazingly self-centered ones roam taking one bite out of every girlish candy in the box.

But the ones that especially piss me off are those that sample different flavors of kids.

You see I don't believe we should treat children like bags of doughnuts.

And so, my simple judgment upon those who do: Death by stake.

Ah hell, let's not discriminate: Death to all vampires by stake!

And, Brother, I got one right here.

Chapter 105

I'd been watching kids pass in pairs and triplets down the hallway when a girl came up and sat on the bench next to me.

She was about 10 in green sweatshirt and jeans cutoffs and tennis shoes without socks. She had a troubled look as she sat down just a few inches from me. I realized she was getting in line. Her eyebrows were hitched and her mouth serious.

"Are you waiting for Mrs. St. George?" she turned and asked me. I could see she was hoping I wasn't.

"Yes," I said. "You need to see her, too?"

The girl nodded.

"Don't worry about me, you can see her right away, if you like," I said.

The girl nodded.

"Troubles?" I asked.

Then she really looked at me. Finally she nodded again.

"What's your name?" I asked.

"Tessa," she admitted.

We sat in silence.

"I need to see her because I'm leaving this place," said Tessa.

"Oh?" I said.

"Yes. I hate it. I hate it here. I'm going."

"But do you have a place to go?" I asked.

Then Tessa looked quickly down at her knees. Her lips trembled a bit. She was doing her best to keep it in.

"I thought of going back to my family, but they won't let me."

"You have a family then? And you're here?"

"My Mom and Dad fight. My Dad tried to kill my Mom. So I got put here. My Dad's in jail. My older brother he's still with my Mom because he's twenty and the courts can't do anything to him. But I can't. The courts said my Mom wasn't fit. She does drugs and stuff. I was in five foster homes, but they don't like me."

"Would you want to go back if you could?"

"No," admitted Tessa. She said it without hesitation such that it was easy to overlook the statement's gravity.

"But I hate it here. I'm leaving. I'm telling Mrs. St. George. But nobody believes me. But I'm going." Tessa looked at me her chin up in defiance.

"I believe you, Tessa," I said.

"You do?" she asked. She now looked me over, her eyes stopping briefly upon my cane companion.

"Yes."

"Why?"

That made me smile. "Oh, because, your troubles are real. Your feelings are real. Just because you're young doesn't mean you don't have the same feelings I have. I would want to leave, if I were in your shoes. But because you're young, you have fewer things you can do about your problems."

"None," she said. "But leave..."

"And you know even that won't be easy, don't you?"

Tessa nodded. She continued nodding as she looked down in her lap. Then she began to cry in earnest.

I don't know how, but lately it seemed I was one big tear-magnet.

Tessa pulled out a Kleenex, wiped her eyes, and put the crumpled wad down beside her in the small space between us. I edged away ever so discreetly. For safety.

"Your troubles are real, Tessa. I know it. I can see it," I said. I scooted back a little more from the tear-dampened Kleenex. I didn't want to touch it and have her see me shrivel and die right in front of her.

"What can I do?" said Tessa to her knees.

"Tessa, I don't have any good news. You're stuck. From now until you're 18 or 20, when you can get away and take care of yourself, you can't do much. Like so many, you just have to stick it out until your old enough. But your problems and feelings they're as important as any adult's. Your problems are real and difficult. And you don't have to believe anybody who tells you different. Your problems and feeling are real and important. I know it. And you know it."

"Sometimes people treat me like I have toy feelings or something. You know? Like they're small and don't count, because their mine, and I'm only eleven."

"You're eleven?" I said. So was my daughter. I quickly tried to shuffle this recognition away.

"Tessa, can I ask you something?"

"Sure," said Tessa. She reached beside her for her deadly hanky and then snuffled into the wadded ball.

"When you go, will your problems and feelings, will they be over?"

"Only if I kill myself," said Tessa.

Oh, my goodness, kids can be such incredibly clear-minded existentialists.

"Please don't do that, you just need to be your brave self and keep on until you're old enough to create your own world outside of here."

"But, really," I persisted, "If you leave, just leave mind you, will your problems and feelings be gone?"

Tessa thought a moment. "No, I guess they'd just go with me."

Tessa sat in deep thought nearly a minute. I sat silently having to respect that.

"So I guess I'll stay," she said.

"Tessa, you're a very bright girl," I said.

Tessa tried a smile.

"What's your name?" she asked.

"Bill."

"Why are you here? Are you looking to adopt somebody? Is that why you're going to see Mrs. St. George?"

"No," I said, "I'm here to kill evil things that might bother you."

"Kill things? How?"

"With this," I smiled, raising my cane.

Tessa laughed.

"Cool!" she said.

Chapter 106

"Tessa, can I give you a piece of advice?" I asked.

"I guess so," replied Tessa. I could see her beginning to cloak up her mind to protect herself from the adult world.

"Don't despair," I said.

Tessa looked at me. She'd been prepared for a long bit of oratory.

Tessa's mouth turned sideways, "I guess I don't get it. I don't know what that means."

"It is hard to understand," I said. "Would you like to hear a poem about it?"

"Is it a hard one?" asked Tessa, as if I were going to ask her to memorize something.

I laughed, "Not at all."

"Okay," she said, still a bit hesitant.

Derry's Vampire

"This poem I call Rant of Joy, Ode to Despair."

Rant of Joy, Ode to Despair

Do you know what despair is?
No, it's not a bucket of sadness your hang around your neck
on an ever tightening noose.

It's just a gray tinge to the mattress.

It's what happens when the string breaks on the pearl necklace
and every shiny one bounces away on its own power
leaving powerless you

Despair, loved one, is not a feeling.
Despair, lovey, is a seeing.

So, let's stand together here in this abyss.
Stand next to me. I'm about as warm and human
as the rest of the monsters down here.

Give old Frankenstein a shove and stand next to me.
I love you. Come out of your despair.

Yes, this abyss is so deep, soo deep
it is actually inside us.

I will sing a little song, hum a little ditty of love.

Put down that note pad! Stop rewriting the definitions of despair!
I won't give you a rock to suck on and call it water.

There is real water in the world.
There is real joy. I know! I've felt it! You can too with
a little practice. Now, get down and do your joy pushups
One two one two

It will come to you.

When I finished my poem, I looked at Tessa who was watching my face very intently. I smiled.

"Okay," she said.

Chapter 107

Derry's office door opened beside us and Mr. and Mrs. Moyer stepped out, looking a bit relieved that the interview was over. Mr. Moyer shook Derry's hand with a grateful smile, and Mrs. Moyer raised her hand from her purse almost cheerfully. Finished with the leave taking, both walked off much more relaxed, arm in arm.

Derry looked sideways to find the two of us sitting on her bench.

"Tessa, you want to see me?" asked Derry.

Tessa squeezed her wadded Kleenex and looked at me.

"I guess not," she shrugged.

"Bye, Bill," she said as she got up and left. I waved the doggy head of my cane a couple cheery bobs.

"Come back whenever you like," called Derry after her. Tessa nodded without looking back.

"Funny, Tessa comes to see me nearly every day. Complaining. Often threatening to leave. She's a real handful and very needy. There comes a point where I don't know what to say to her."

Derry looked at me with cocked-brow.

"What did you tell her?"

"Nothing she didn't already know," I said.

Chapter 108

"Shall we continue our tour?" I suggested.

"Bill, I don't feel comfortable with this," said Derry.

"You mean leading a vampire around your home ground?"

Derry nodded.

"I understand. I'm part of the unknown, the blackness in the world that you really would rather not be there. No one wants to lead it into their life. I understand."

"Could you, could you just leave?" ventured Derry with an anxious clenching of her jaws. It almost gave me the impression she was worried about hurting my feelings.

I shook my head smiling.

"No, Derry, the only way of getting rid of the unknown, is making it known. It's too late. It's too late to look the other way."

"Why?" said Derry a bit vexed.

"Because if you look the other way, someday there'll just be another vampire standing there."

Derry's face clouded with a great deal of pain, a pleading weight below her eyes.

"The only thing I can say," I said resolutely, "Is that if you face me, Derry, you'll find you aren't alone."

"Left alone is what I want to be!" protested Derry. A couple of passing children looked left at Derry as she said this, but kept walking.

"Of course," I said, then I laughed, "Too late!"

"Gah, a vampire with a sense of humor," cursed Derry.

Then I really laughed.

And the passing children actually stopped to look at me hopefully.

Chapter 109

Derry walked me up a flight of stairs.

"You may as well see the dorm rooms, I've got to check on something in the infirmary."

The second floor was a long linoleum tiled alley. A resolute line of tall doors stood at attention on both sides of the hall, all open.

"This was a children's hospital in its last incarnation. The second floor rooms were private rooms, but converted pretty well into dorm rooms, except they're not so private."

I looked into several of the open doors as we passed. The rooms were smallish, but large enough for two beds and two desks to stand without touching. A single window looked out on the grounds. Some rooms had walls well-tacked with posters, rock bands, models, the icons of youth. Others had little on the walls except a few squiggly drawings made by small hands. A stuffed animal or two usually haunted the bed or chairs of such rooms. For the most part, the chambers were clean, with just a few socks and shirts spread on the floor.

"Pretty nice," I said.

"Thanks, we work with the kids on respecting the others in your room. Because they share the same situation. Some can understand they need to help each other. Others can't."

At the far end of the hall a lanky man, bony, with an Icabod Crane stature, stood leaning on a mop. He was talking with a tight grin to several boys standing before him. He wore black overalls, saggy and torn in the back pockets. The pail beside the man was nearly black with dirty water. The only water on the floor was under the mop head, propping up the spindly man, as he grinned and grinned at these boys. I noticed the boys were looking at their feet as they talked.

145

"Who's that?" I asked Derry as we neared.

"That's Fred, our janitor. Fred's quite an institution here. Certain boys seem to flock to him. There's always two or three asking him questions."

"The infirmary is at the end of the hall here," said Derry, "Hey, Fred!"

Derry's call brought the janitor's head turning quickly toward us.

"Hey, Mrs. St. George," said Fred, flashing the same toothy, false-grin toward us. Then Fred looked my way.

Something in his eyes tightened on seeing me.

"Hey, Fred," I said as I passed following Derry.

I was glad Derry didn't look back. She would have seen in Fred's eyes that he didn't like seeing me at all.

That's okay, I didn't like seeing him either.

Chapter 110

We came to a locked door beside a small frosted window. There was another bench beside this door.

"Here we are," said Derry to the door.

"Derry, is Fred a recent hire?" I asked.

"No, he's been here since...Well, actually he came with the building. He was a janitor for the children's hospital 12 years ago, then helped us during the conversion. He lives downstairs in a backroom near the main plant and laundry. He's as much an institution here as our furnace."

I nodded, relieved that Fred at least wasn't one of Hierpat's little helpers.

Chapter 111

Derry fumbled with the key.

"You lock the infirmary?" I asked.

Derry paused and thought a moment. "Yes. We have a nurse in attendance at all times. We also have prescription drugs on site, so we keep the door locked. Besides there's the question of contagion. We don't want little unexpected visitors seeing those who've got the chicken pox and such."

I nodded.

"Bill, do you mind waiting here as I go in alone? I'll be short. I just need to check a few things."

"Sure," I said. Once again I sat down on the waiting bench beside the locked door. I looked out the window as Derry disappeared with the door closing.

I put my hands between my legs and twiddled thumbs, musing.

Certain animals are good at waiting, spiders, ticks, leeches, vampires...

I realized I now probably knew where Derry's son was. She had mentioned he'd become ill after the attack. And here Derry was visiting a locked infirmary at her place of work. Keeping me at bay.

Humans aren't so hard to figure.

As, unfortunately, my vampire fellows will also tell you.

Chapter 112

That afternoon I was treated to a marvelous experience.

Derry had walked me out behind the orphanage to a play field. A small enclosed area was filled with climbing structures and swings for the smaller kids, all visible from the street. But beside it was a large open plot of grass, sunny and scuffed bare in patches by many feet. I could see the tracing of a baseball diamond in one corner and goal posts of a football field. As many as two dozen kids, boys and girls in shorts and T-shirts, were running wild chasing a soccer ball.

The shrieks, howls, and yelling was fantastic, but good-natured. I saw fast dashes, hard kicks, and falls where the faller lay laughing. Smaller kids who'd taken a tumble were helped up by older ones.

"Fun," I said to Derry, but she'd already left me at the edge of the play field.

Her shoes were off. And she was running.

To my amazement I watched Derry join the gamboling pack, laughing and chasing a kicked ball. Kid's yelled in recognition on seeing her enter the game. The play grew just a bit more intense. Husky boys dived heroically to stop Derry from scoring. Pursuing girls laughed, shrieked, and began pulling sweatshirts to slow their opponents. Derry was laughing and directing the traffic of her quickly adopted team. Littler ones were running with all the might their short legs could muster.

"Here! Here! Here!" shouted Derry calling for a pass.

Glorious fun and commotion.

It was funny to see the director of this orphanage disappear completely. She was gone, the hassle, fun, and competition between a tribe of running young ones was all I saw. And Derry running barefoot, sun on her flying hair, in the midst of them.

Marvelous sight for an old vampire.

Finally the game ended with Derry passing out hugs to players from both teams glued to her side. All were a bit wobbly, gulping, and breathless.

Shining faces coming in from ventures on a sea of grass.

I remembered such play. And envied Derry that she was still a part.

Chapter 113

Derry bid good-bye to the players on the field, giving work as an excuse from breaking off from them. The kids hesitated then wandered back to their orbits around a traipsing ball.

Derry picked up her shoes from where they'd been kicked off.

She sobered a bit as she came back to me.

"What?" she said, looking at me quizzically.

"Nothing," I smiled.

"Why are you looking at me like that?"

"I can't tell you," I laughed.

"You've never seen anybody play soccer before?" asked Derry.

"Hmmm," I said, "Maybe not as thoroughly as that."

"I did kind of get into it, didn't I?" said Derry, looking back over her shoulder at the running hubbub.

"Maybe," I said.

Derry laughed at herself.

Chapter 114

Derry had walked me back into her office. It was a large open chamber with wide window on the playground. One wall was lined

150

with books fallen on their sides or resting tilted at exhausted angles. Small photographs of kids and hand drawings papered the walls like huge mounted butterflies. I sat in one of two easy chairs, fatly-padded and comfortable, facing Derry. Derry at first checked a few phone messages and a ledger before folding her hands and looking at me. Once again, even before she opened her mouth, I felt an outsider.

"What do you think about children? I mean, as a vampire. How do you see them? Why would you want to help me? Why would you care whether my kids become vampires or not?" said Derry.

"Old lessons," I said. "There are old lessons about kids that one learns. Lessons learned as an adult, and learned early as a kid. I was a father, you know? I wrote a poem about it."

"Do your poem," commanded Derry. She was skeptical of my poetry now that she knew its source.

"I call this poem An Essay."

An Essay

Oh parents,
every gardener knows that you can't make the rose grow
by shouting at it

that children are like glass mirrors
it takes a lot of work to keep them clean
and after years of work you still just
see yourself

Derry's Vampire

If you carry a little ticking bomb in your heart
your children will carry little ticking bombs
in their hearts
waiting to go off
if you rage with a chain saw
your children will either be afraid of chain saws
or join the chain saw brigade

Kids are cute and cuddly
when they're small but when they're teenagers
there you are
they have exactly your problems the problems you never solved
and you haven't got the answers and all you can offer
is the same buckets of glue that you stuck your feet in
and now clumpf around on
and you think it's okay
when they're telling you it isn't okay

and they're right
AND THAT MAKES YOU MAD

Do you drink the rosy wine of mystery under the Easter Egg yellow
moon?
So do they
Do you hear the moaning moose bellow of distanced sex-mates
that perks up your antlers?
So do they

Derry's Vampire

Do you know the harrowing blankness of thinking about what it's
like to be dead
have your body dissolve into the gooey earth, have
mother nature forget you, feel the real emptiness between stars?
They've thought about it, maybe at about ten
or eleven. Don't think your children aren't pioneers
in these chilly realms at a tender age

kids are existentialists
they live on barren asteroids, they'll eat popcorn from under
the sofa, they'll cut angle worms in half
with a butcher knife just to see the wince
unless you give them something better

Am I lecturing you just like your dear old dad, just like his dear old
dad, just like HIS dear old dad, just like his dear DEAD old dad, just
like Ug the cave Dad?
Are you going to pass it on?

They give you the gift of giggles
They give you the gift of lost kid fun, amazing card tricks that stake
up our heart like circus tent poles with pride, the camaraderie of
learning to bake an apple pie, tragedy in a burnt finger,
the shock of crayons on the walls
the howls of grief
the jigs of joy and hopscotch

they give you life

life anew

Make it a good one.

"And how does your bar crowd react to that?" asked Derry.

"Oh, a smattering of applause, but mostly guilty silence," I said.

Derry looked at me a long moment.

And again I saw something deeply in her eyes that I wanted.

Chapter 115

I'd been shadowing Derry all day, watching her tread the routine tracks of her job. I'd tried to be as non-intrusive as possible, so that she could ignore me if she chose. Except it was probably an impossible choice. Even as she talked to staff, advising Heniretta, phoning Hilda, she stole glances at me, just to pin down my position in the room. I felt kind of like a sideshow come to town. At about 3:30, Derry suggested we take a break.

"Let's get some coffee. There's a place across the park."

"Right on," I said.

Derry laughed, "That was very sixties..."

"Would that be 1960's or 1860's?" I asked.

"I don't remember much of the 1860's," said Derry with an amused sarcasm.

I didn't say that I did.

Derry and I descended to the lobby, then walked the drive out to the street fronting the park.

"The coffee shop's over there," said Derry pointing through some trees to a small cave-like door across the park's expanse.

She descended the curb and started across the street, lined with parked cars, me one step behind. There was no traffic. About a hundred yards away I heard a car start up with a roar, then pull out into the lane. I looked right to make sure there was enough time to make the crossing.

A black BMW was picking up speed, coming right at us. Its windows deeply tinted, I could only make out the form of the driver and a passenger.

Derry stopped mid-street saying, "What?" as the car lowered into a bull charge.

"Move Derry!" I said.

Derry froze in the center of the street. The bumper of the on-coming car was crossing the white line.

I jumped forward and gave Derry a shove.

Then she ran. In three short strides, she made it between two parked cars and up on the sidewalk, safe behind their metal protection.

Unswerving, the car accelerated straight at me.

I jumped so the bumper wouldn't clip me at the legs. I went high enough that my shoulder slapped the car roof, spinning me like a top. The car barreled on under me. I fell to the ground as it continued at high speed down the block.

If I'd been a human, my little car somersault probably would have broken my neck.

The black BMW squealed right around the corner and disappeared.

"Bill!" gasped Derry, now leaning at my shoulder. I sat up slowly, seeing there was practically no damage to my leather coat. That's the great thing about leather.

"Are you all right?" asked Derry, her brow furrowed.

"Yes," I said.

Derry looked at me uneasily.

"It was your husband, wasn't it?" I said.

Derry nodded again. I didn't ask who else was in the car.

"Is he that desperate for the kids that he'd try to kill me?" Derry asked herself aloud. Her voice was quaking and she gulped in breath.

I stood up. I felt fine. In fact, I felt great. I'd picked up the trail and was on the hunt.

However, the event for Derry was less than exhilarating, she was faint and shaken.

Chapter 116

I walked Derry to the little coffee shop, where we stood in line and ordered cappachino's. We said nary a word as we waited, I suppose pretending an ordinary life on the outside as raging conflicts of our emotional lives waged within, like most people. Derry stole quick glances at me, her face unhappy and tense as I ordered.

We sat down in a secluded corner. We sipped coffee without a word.

"How can he be so desperate? That's not the man I knew. He was incapable."

"Men and women are capable of anything," I said, "It's just we're always surprised by it."

"Why would he try to kill me and risk jail? Surely that was a stupid attempt. How could it not attract attention? 'Man Runs Over Own Wife For Kids' what else could the headline be? Is he that angry at me? What did I do?"

"Nothing," I said. "Something's happened to him. I expect."

"What?" Derry swallowed and peered intently.

It was too much bad news in a single jolt.

"Perhaps he wasn't aiming at you," I said evasively.

"You mean he was just trying to scare me?"

"Mmmm," I grunted, meaning no.

"What then?"

"Maybe it was about me," I said.

"You mean he's trying to kill you in a fit of jealous rage? Something like that?"

"Something like that. Perhaps he was trying to eliminate the competition."

"No, he's seen you once for only a few seconds, that doesn't add up. How could he know you are involved or mean anything to me?"

I shrugged.

"I'll have to look into it," I said.

"But, Derry," I continued, "An attempt on your life does make sense. Eventually your son would turn up and be handed over to someone. We need to be especially careful. You see that now, don't you?"

Derry nodded grudgingly.

"Derry, I need to stay close by at all times. Can you trust me to let me do that?" I asked.

Again she nodded. But this time the bitterness in her face was heavy and her mouth almost an icicle.

I told Derry we should call it a day and she go home and rest till the next morning.

I walked Derry to her apartment building, tall and flower-covered. I insisted on walking her right up to the door. I could see she felt crowded as if forced to wear an unwanted piece of clothing. I told her to rest, she'd be safe there.

The door closed without Derry replying.

I waited until I heard the lock.

Chapter 117

When Derry's door closed, I turned and headed home. I needed to go pick up my squirt gun. I planned to spend the night in the surroundings of Derry's apartment building, just in case.

I walked home, treading the perpendicular paths of city streets to my lair. It was a big apartment building, well-kept. Old. Comfortable. Importantly, no concierge or doorman.

I need the freedom to slip in and out late at night.

I'd no sooner put the key in my lock than I heard my phone going off.

I walked over and picked up the receiver without turning on the lights.

"*Ecoute, quite la femme ou morir*," said an ancient gravelly voice in the receiver.

"*Qui c'est?*" I asked.

"*Rest avec cette femme, ce'st la morte pour toi*," insisted the voice.

"*Qui c'est?*" I repeated.

"Hierpat."

This was the first time I'd heard the voice of my ancient enemy.

"Fuck you," I shouted and put down the receiver.

I found I was trembling with rage.

Gee, I liked the way things were going.

Chapter 118

When Derry opened her apartment door the next morning she found me sitting on a window sill at the end of the hall. I rose, said good morning, and was answered only by Derry's unhappy grimace. I followed her down the stairs and walked her to the Sunnyrock Home for Children. Derry didn't have much to say to me. Again I spent the day sitting on benches outside of doors as Derry worked. I spent a good deal of time thinking about Derry.

Nothing untoward happened that day.

Or the next.

The third day, Derry opened her door early and invited me in for breakfast.

As I sat down at her kitchen table to coffee and scrambled eggs, I said I was much obliged.

"The neighbors complained," said Derry, sitting down across from me.

"They want to know who the strange man lurking around is."

"Want me to tell them?" I said, smiling, raising my cup.

"Say what? You're my pet vampire?" asked Derry.

"Something like that," I said.

"You would," she said. Derry almost smiled. Then she let go a deep sigh.

"What are you doing, are you sitting up in my hallway all night?"

"No, I'm just around. Watching. I come early into the hall to meet you is all."

"And the rest of the time, you're just out there? All night?"

"All night," I confirmed.

"In the darkness?" asked Derry.

"That's how night works," I said lightly.

Derry pursed her lips and looked at me.

"Must you?" she pleaded.

"Yes," I said.

"It can't be very comfortable," said Derry.

I shrugged. Personal comfort wasn't an issue of mine, I had other fun, bloodthirsty pursuits.

"Derry, you know why I'm here."

"The neighbor's are complaining, they're going to call the cops. There's going to be no end of hassles, if you persist."

"I can stay out of the building," I suggested.

"What? You'll sneak around the dumpsters like the rest of the alley cats?"

"Derry," I said, kindly, "Have mercy. You're not very flattering of me."

I saw that when I said 'have mercy' Derry had blinked.

"What are we doing?" Derry said to the ceiling.

I took another drink of my coffee. I knew Derry was working up to something and I had to let her get to it herself.

"Bill, I'm terrified," said Derry.

"I know," I said. "But I must be here for you."

"Okay, okay!" Derry exclaimed in exasperation, "You can stay on the couch. I'm not letting you use my son's room, and I'm not letting you into mine. I'm locking the doors!"

I accepted my new sleeping arrangement with a bow of the head.

"Thank you, Derry," I said.

As if in pain, Derry put her hand to her forehead and left the room.

I finished my scrambled eggs.

Chapter 119

Derry was getting used to me accompanying her, something like a bodyguard. However, she was careful to keep a good distance between herself and me.

Walking to the Home that morning, Derry informed me that the day's routine would be a little different today.

"We're taking a group to a playground on the other side of the park. A small picnic outing. I don't have much happening today, so I'll be going along. We try to do it once a week for the smaller kids."

"You don't want me to go?" I asked.

"No, I do," said Derry, "You can help watch the kids. I just wanted to let you know."

I realized Derry was acting as if I were one of her staff.

I nodded.

Chapter 120

"Are we going to the park today?" he shouted as he sprinted across the lobby to us. Derry had just opened the orphanage front door when the blond haired boy, Kelly, slammed into her legs and held her like an apron.

"Well," laughed Derry looking down, "I think we are. Do you want to go?"

"Are you going to be with me all day?" asked Kelly looking up beaming.

"Sure, Kelly, I'll be there, and I think we'll be leaving in about a half hour." The overjoyed five-year-old looked my way.

"Are you going, too?" he asked me.

"Yup, I think so," I said.

"Great! Can I play with your cane?"

I laughed. "No, I think I need to use it."

"Now, go see Hilda, I think she's going with us. Tell her to get the other kids ready. Then we're off," said Derry, smiling down.

"Okay!"

With that Kelly jogged away down a hallway.

"Well, that was quite a greeting," I said.

"Yes, you never know what's going to hit you when you open a door around here."

"So the park is soon?" I said.

"About a half hour. Can you wait down here? I have a couple things to do, and then we'll gather the kids. We just walk over. It's about a half-mile down to the spot where the kids like to play."

"Okay," I said. I went to sit on a lobby sofa as Derry walked away. I knew she wanted to be away from me for some reason and I didn't want to press it.

A half hour later, a rambling troupe of four and five-year-olds, all walking with brightly colored lunch boxes, entered in a line of twos, with just a little running and shoving, as you might expect with any line of chimps.

Hilda, in a pink sweater and sky blue smock, was directing traffic, trying to drive the kids in an organized clump through the lobby. Hugging a white blanket under her arm, she was carrying a small paper bag that wagged from her other raised hand as she pointed out the lobby door.

"Please, boys and girls, that way! You know where the park is!"

"Bill, you're going with us, today?" she called.

"Wouldn't miss it," I said.

I got up smiling and waved my cane toward the door. This caught the attention of the many small puzzling minds, which began moving small bodies by consensus in that direction.

"Be right there!" I heard called behind me. It was Derry's voice.

In a few fast paces, Derry was with us, receiving the recognizing calls of "Mrs. St. George!" and other greetings.

Looking down, it was strange to have a world talking to you that was only three feet high.

Kelly ran over and claimed Derry's hand. He began tugging her along toward the door.

"All right, let's go!" shouted Hilda. "Derry, we've got fourteen here in all."

"Okay, launch," commanded Derry.

With that Hilda stepped out the door, walking backward, coaxing out our little parade.

"This looks fun," I said.

"Ah, the voice of inexperience," laughed Derry, "Just don't offer to carry anyone piggyback unless you can carry fourteen."

"Only fourteen?" I laughed.

Sunny, warm, the morning dew just gone, it was a great day for growing flowers and taking kids to the park. The grass was sloping away green and thick as bear fur. Asphalt walks were warm with thick puddles of sun and tree shade. People in shorts were walking their dogs. An elderly couple with china white hair, the man pear-shaped in sweatshirt, the woman in beige shorts and very white shoes, was jogging carrying tennis rackets and a ball can. A park worker in drab brown was leaning on a rake as he watched a nearby sprinkler spritz water into a flower bed. The children headed in a wave toward the sprinkler, but Hilda squawked.

"Nope! Nope! Nope! Out of the water! Out!"

I watched with amusement as our running pack slowed, then passed the water source untouched, looking over their shoulders regretfully as they headed deeper into the park.

"Thanks, Hilda!" called Derry, "Close call! We don't want them totally quenched and soaking before we get there."

"Why not?" I asked.

Derry laughed. "Maybe on the way back..."

Hilda ran taking up the point.

I walked beside Derry, strolling easily with a steady click of my cane.

Kelly was sticking close, nearly hanging from Derry's hand like a purse.

"Will you go on the slide with me when we get there?" he asked, looking up.

Derry smiled, "Maybe, but I'm a little old for that old slide."

"Please?" said Kelly.

"We'll see," said Derry.

I was enjoying walking beside Derry. Her hair clipped back with a comb, wearing only a pale rose lipstick as makeup, she looked at ease as she called out sights to the group. She had on what must have been her safari clothes, a white blouse, ivory pants of light fabric, and white tennis shoes. She and Hilda exchanged hand signals as they directed traffic, reminding me a little of the infantry combat hand signs you see in World War II movies. Obviously, shepherding kids through the park required teamwork. Derry looked momentarily carefree, involved in the daily minutia of an organized walk in the park and I could see working now with kids was good for her.

I took a deep breath and felt the ancient air of Spring enter me.

After a longish walk, we came to an open glade lined in the background with the brush and deeper verdure of the park. Swings and play equipment stood, braced for attention, in a distant sand pit. The kids dispersed on the run with the occasional cartwheel, high-stepping, and top twirls and falls that kids perform so professionally. And watching their fun, I'd say the pay was good.

Hilda, Derry, and I repaired up a slope and set up camp. Hilda spread her white blanket on the crisp green lawn, checked with Derry on the official time for lunch, then left to supervise the play structure antics. Kelly was now tugging Derry in the direction of the slides, and I sat to watch our little circus.

As I looked out across the green slope, I saw many brightly colored dandelions. Free to grow.

Chapter 121

Amid the occasional tumble and call for help, Derry, Hilda, and I had an easy time of it. The kids were entertained by each other and only needed infrequent suggestions for things to do. Hilda had led games of Frozen Tag, Red-rover, and Ring-Around-the-Rosy. I remembered this last one from the time of the plague.

Derry enlisted me as It in a game of Hide and Seek. Arms up, I gamboled around the play structures like a nearly blind abominable snowman, chasing kids that were still too young to know how to hide themselves. I'd look behind a rock to find a squatting threesome, but carefully tumbled before I caught anyone. I reached into the concrete tube, but never quite far enough to catch a scooting leg. I wailed and pouted, and waved my arms over my head. At one point, Kelly jumped up on the edge of the sandpit, stuck out his tongue, and wagged his hands as ears at me. I roared in anguish, which sent the little herd squealing and giggling to escape.

I looked and Derry was laughing at me with her hand over her mouth. Hilda was shaking her head and laughing.

"You're catching no one fast," shouted Derry.

"Argh, tell me!" I shouted. Finally, I grabbed my chest where my heart should have been and fell to a fake heart-attack.

Derry announced Hide and Seek was over, It was dead.

The little group crowded around me with interest, then after a few moments, started to throw grass on my face.

"Even a proper burial," laughed Derry to Hilda.

"Time for lunch," called Hilda.

Derry and Kelly pulled on my hands to help me stand up.

But my weight was too great.

I had to get up myself.

Chapter 122

We ate lunch with the kids prospecting in their lunch boxes and nibbling. I sat with Derry, Hilda, and the ever-present Kelly, squashed like a bookend to Derry's side.

After several attempts, Derry finally shucked Kelly off to go play the final hour with the group.

I sat with Derry, and Hilda, who was now plainly tired, in the relaxing sun. We watched the kid pack and other park pedestrians move in and out of view.

"This is kind of a good job," I joked, "And you get paid for this?"

"Sure," said Derry.

"As long as Henrietta's numbers add up," said Hilda blithely.

"How do you get paid?" asked Derry suddenly.

I looked over at her.

"Like you, the pay is the job," I said evenly.

"And you like your work?" asked Derry.

"Like you," I said, "It's the best."

But instead of insult, my voice had betrayed regret.

"What is it that you do, Bill?" asked Hilda, perking up.

"Well, I walk around and professionally carry a cane," I smiled.

"Bill is into protecting people," broke in Derry.

Hilda's face took on concern.

"Are things that bad between you and your husband, Derry?"

169

"We're not sure," she said.

I though it best to remain discreet.

"I'm sorry to hear that," said Hilda.

"Well, best be getting our little tribe back on the trail," said Derry abruptly.

Hilda stood and went to the structure to gather the clan.

I stood up next to Derry, both brushing grass and leaves from ourselves.

We walked down to Hilda and the kid assembly.

"Derry, I count thirteen," said Hilda, frowning.

"Who's missing?" asked Derry loudly over the heads of all.

I looked at the faces.

A little girl with red hair stuck out an arm and pointed. "Kelly went over there!"

I looked across the park and there at the edge of the trees was Kelly walking away hand in hand with another man.

"I'll take care of it," I said. I gripped my cane and began a quick jog across the park.

The man was in a black raincoat with lumpy fedora. He was talking to Kelly as he pulled the boy by the hand into the thicker stand of trees. Kelly's feet were now barely touching the ground as they hurried.

When I reached the pair, there were a few intervening trees, but I knew Derry, Hilda, and the kids could still see us.

"Hold up there," I said. I slowed to a walk. The man in the black raincoat stopped suddenly, a little as if an arrow had hit his back. He looked furtively over his shoulder. He was an older man with beadled looks and grizzled chin. Kelly was now trying to wring his hand free, his face wincing.

I stepped forward and pulled Kelly's hand away. I set him running back to the group.

I gave a friendly wave back across the field to Derry.

The old man was looking strangely at me now, his mouth working dryly.

I pushed his back against a tree so that he was hidden from the distant group.

I said, "You're lucky they can see us, or I'd be staking you right now with this." I raised my cane so that he could see its laughing doggy head.

Then I bopped him between the eyes and his feet went out from under him.

I left him sitting against a tree unconscious as I walked back to Derry.

Chapter 123

Lecturing Kelly, who was now in tears, Derry was white-faced and urgent in her instructions to all about talking to strangers. The whole group of young ones stood morose and silent.

"If Bill hadn't gone out and got you, who knows where you'd be right now!" said Derry. Kelly was silent, tears streaming down his face.

"We were all scared by it, " I said. "I think we should just go back Home."

Stiff and unhappy, the kids began moving in a group almost glacially.

"You'll hear more about this when we get back," said Derry.

She was upset. Hilda moved closed-face to the front of the group.

"Thank you, Bill," said Derry to me just before we took up the rear.

I nodded.

"What did you say to him?" asked Derry, looking back across the field.

"There wasn't much to say," I said.

"Did you..?" and Derry made a motion as if she were stabbing a broom handle.

"No," I said.

"Thank, God," said Derry.

"Was he...?" asked Derry.

I looked at her.

"Yes."

Chapter 124

We returned to the Home, an unhappy group. An intruder had spoiled the fun. Hilda took all off to different destinations. Kelly walked away as if heading for a firing squad.

Derry watched the retreating group, glanced at me, then begged leave because she needed to do some work alone in her office. I agreed to wait for her return in the lobby.

"Thanks again, Bill," said Derry.

"I'm glad I was there," I said.

"Me too." Derry made an immense frown.

She walked off without saying another word to me.

Chapter 125

That evening as Derry knit her house key into her apartment door, she hesitated. She looked at me standing beside her, then to the door.

Finally, she pushed the door open with an elbow and stood back waiting.

I entered the darkened space of her apartment.

Then the lights went on.

"I'll be just a minute," called Derry, heading for her room, "Then I'll try to fix us a little dinner."

"Thanks," I said.

Derry disappeared perhaps to visit the bathroom or change clothes, but I suspected more importantly to escape the awkwardness of me being there.

I sat on the couch, relaxed a bit.

Derry came in a few minutes later in untucked flannel shirt and sweat-pants, talking as she headed for the kitchen.

"I think I've got some lettuce for salad, I often bake a potato, with butter. Sound okay for you?"

"Sure," I called. "Maybe I can help?"

I got up and went into the kitchen.

"Only if you wash dishes," laughed Derry. A humped pile of unclean dishes was slouching in the sink.

"You cook, I'll clean," I said.

I rolled up my sleeves and began running hot water in the sink. Soon the detergent was bubbling as I stacked the dirty plates for take off.

Derry walked back and forth in the kitchen finding food and utensils. As she washed, chopped, and baked our meal, I began washing, rinsing, and drying.

We both relaxed with light tasks. I asked where a few things should be put away. Derry pointed and explained.

"Funny," said Derry. "I'd forgotten what sharing the kitchen was like. My husband left me a year ago. I was feeling a hermit or something. But it's so easy to slip into domesticity."

"Good," I said.

Then Derry's cheeks grew intensely red. And she suddenly had nowhere to place her hands.

I laughed at her.

"Gahh," replied Derry, "Let's just eat, shall we?"

Chapter 126

We'd just finished our repas and were sitting at Derry's little kitchen table.

"So, how do you do it?" asked Derry.

"Do what, exactly?"

"Kill vampires, that's what I need to know now, I suppose."

"First, you have to be prepared to do it," I said.

"I'm not," said Derry flatly.

"Practically nobody is," I concurred.

"Except you," said Derry.

"Yes, me. And if we're lucky, maybe not you."

"What's the preparation?"

"Well, without getting into it too deeply, you must be either very cold-blooded about it."

"Which you are," said Derry.

I nodded, "or very light-hearted. Killing them by surprise almost on a whim."

"Why?"

"Otherwise, they feed on the emotions you generate, grow stronger. It weakens you, you become easier to kill, emotionally."

"I don't sound like a good candidate. Do you always use your cane?"

"No. Basically, I kill two ways, with my cane. As you saw in the alley. The other with this."

I reached into my pocket and took out a small capped vial, the size of a tiny perfume capsule. I put the stoppered vial on the table where it stood like a small unlit candle.

"What's inside?" asked Derry with equal repugnance and fascination.

"The liquid is simply a child's tears. Should it touch a vampire, it kills him instantly."

"It would kill you instantly?"

"Yes," I said.

"I mix it with water and squirt it on vampires," I said.

"That's it? A child's tears? I had the impression that vampires were practically invulnerable, and yet, if they touch a child's tears, they die? You'd think they'd be dying all the time, if it's as easy as that."

"It seems common, but how often do you come in contact with a child's tears?"

Derry thought a moment.

"Rarely," admitted Derry.

"I want you to take that, Derry. Keep it on you at all times. In case you ever need it," I said.

"For any reason," I said. Then I looked my meaning at her.

Derry stood up and cleared her plate from the table. I stood up and cleared mine. I washed and rinsed the dishes and put them away. Derry left the room.

When I turned to leave the kitchen, the little vial was gone.

Chapter 127

The next morning, I woke early on Derry's couch. I got up and washed, then went into the kitchen to fix a little breakfast.

I was setting the table for two, with the coffee and toast made and eggs and bacon frying, when Derry appeared.

She stepped out of her room fully dressed, looking around a bit suspiciously.

"In here," I called. "Do you eat eggs every morning?"

Derry hesitated then walked in seeing breakfast nearly ready. She mustered a smile.

"No, I never eat them, actually."

"Why yesterday?" I asked.

"Oh, I figured you were a high cholesterol kind of person."

"That's a new low for my personal esteem," I said. "I like to think of myself as *high octane*, practically *atomic*."

"Like radioactive waste, with a half-life of a million years," laughed Derry.

"Precisely," I said.

"And after you die, archaeologists a million years from now can dig you up and find your fossilized heart still beating..." said Derry.

"That's the plan," I laughed.

As we had coffee, Derry told me that she'd have several meetings in a row with prospective couples that afternoon. I'd have to do a lot of waiting. I said that was okay. I'd think of something to do.

There was definitely someone I wanted to check out.

Chapter 128

The afternoon sun hot on my back, I rapt my cane against the door three times. I looked back down the stairs to see if anyone was on the street. The sidewalks were empty with the black BMW shining in the driveway like a huge slug.

I hadn't seen anyone in the windows as I'd stood watching from across the street.

Derry's husband opened the door.

The pallid complexion of his squat face, the haggard strain around his eyes and cheeks, his red hair standing up in a crewcut, all betrayed his sudden look of terror. I saw all I needed to see as he slammed the door shut again.

For his short career as a vampire, someone had educated him. He recognized and knew what I was.

Death in his doorway.

Chapter 129

I went to my apartment and transferred a few things to Derry's. A few things for my personal comfort and daily ablutions, a few props I used on the hunt. Things I might need ready at hand. I was glad Derry wasn't with me for I think she would have had trouble with me so conspicuously moving in. If we somehow managed to grow used to each other, we could compare shavers later.

I went back to the Sunnyrock Home for Children and waited the rest of the afternoon. I tried to decide how to handle the situation with Derry. I now had an avenue I might follow to get to Hierpat. Derry's husband.

Right now, Hierpat seemed way ahead in the game. If Derry were being watched closely, it was likely Hierpat had figured out what I was. This was proven by the reaction of Derry's husband, who'd recognized the danger on his doorstep and slammed the door with all his might. I suspected he'd been told to take a ram at me with his car to check out what I really was. If he'd left human road kill in the street that was no skin off a vampire's nose. But, I'd survived it. And I'd left him safe to consider me a while after taking up his new career as vampire. I'd just left behind four flat tires on his shiny car, staking them one by one with gusto. I'd attend to him later.

But I had to think more on Hierpat. It was likely he was quickly figuring out Derry's situation and the location of her son, as I had. It was a race to see who could figure out who first.

But at least now I might have an avenue that might lead me back to Hierpat. Derry's husband had been converted to a vampire. Who did the converting? And if I found out who did the converting, it might lead me to my enemy...the vampire I most wanted to make a pin cushion.

Chapter 130

Over the next several days, Derry and I set up a routine. I tried to be up before her, dressed, and with the morning kitchen clean and waiting. We'd sit and have coffee together and I'd let Derry discuss her worries about what was going on. I tried little by little to prepare her for things ahead. Things like an attempt that might be made to find and capture her son. And unexpected things that might arrive by surprise out of the blue.

I gave a rather balletic demonstration of how she might thrust with my cane at a vampire's heart. This proved too much for her and she barely spoke to me for the rest of the day.

The next day, in an offhanded way, I suggested that she might want to carry a squirt gun that I could fix up for her. Again, Derry's frown and disapproval were great as if I'd squashed a rodent in front of her on her rug.

She offered to think about it.

And I gave up converting Derry to an instrument of death.

Chapter 131

The morning sun was beaming in the kitchen windows, laying great white newspapers of sunlight on the floor, counters, and chairs. It was cheery and warm, and I'd opened one of the kitchen windows to blow out some of the steam from washing dishes and perking coffee. The air smelled sweet and clean.

I heard a door slide open down the hall. I went over and found Derry's bedroom door had slowly swung wide with the change in air pressure coming from the kitchen. I heard her shower water running from within her room. I walked down to quietly close the door without disturbing her before she discovered it had unnoticed swung free.

As I reached for the doorknob, I saw her room was brilliant with sunlight. The walls were intensely white, as if a searchlight had stilled, trained on them. Prism rays broke from glass knick knacks and bottles on Derry's window sill, stamping rainbow patterns across ceiling and white creases of the sheets on her empty bed. A chair sat like a valet, holding Derry's undergarments and the day's clothes.

Then Derry stepped naked from her bathroom.

She was smiling to herself as she strode in with the turban of a white terry cloth towel wrapped around her head.

I stepped back, so as not to intrude on her, but there was her image reflected in the full length closet mirror.

The sun moved over her body with a curveousness I'd never seen before.

And there, on the white bowl of her hip, was a butterfly mark. An incredibly well-placed birthmark of beauty.

A mark of unbelievable desire.

Chapter 132

If ever you can characterize a vampire as scurrying back to safety, that's what I did. I backed up down the hallway, away from the image of Derry reflected in a mirror, that hateful tool I as a vampire could not look within.

I sat down, weak, at Derry's kitchen table, and looked out the sunny lit window at the blue sky for a long time myself.

For a long time, thinking of my lost self.

Chapter 133

It was funny, but each night that we sat together in her apartment, Derry would ask me one question about something that bothered her. It was like she was climbing a staircase, at the top of which stood the unknown, something perhaps terrifying, and she was taking one hesitant step a night. Some humans refuse knowledge, live like crabs scuttling under rocks, busy, self-contained, projecting the unconscious hardened shell of themselves for safety. Other humans I'd met, people with practically the beauty, skills, and intelligence of deities, accepted self-knowledge in a lightening blast. They radiated self-understanding, which quickly converted to self-love and compassion. But Derry, like most of us, took one step at a time, grew used to it, then summoned the courage to go the next step. And none of us really knew what was at the top of the stairs. Love? Vampires? I couldn't really say.

I wondered what Derry's ESP was telling her. Telling her about me. But I was afraid to ask. A step up I was afraid to take.

"Bill, I don't think you were telling me everything you thought about my husband," started Derry. It was the nightly question.

"No, Derry," I said.

"So," she said hunching her shoulders, "What's the story? He's attacked me. Something he'd never have done."

"Derry, this is hard to say."

"Say it," she commanded.

"He's a vampire now, Derry. There's no denying it. Someone has taken him across. Across to my world."

Derry blinked stunned.

I realized this was a mighty tall step.

"Ohhhh!" Derry put her head back and howled at the ceiling. Tears welled out of the corners of her eyes. She wobbled a bit, then collapsed to her side on the couch. Her face hidden by her arm, she cried, her body shaking in spasms.

I sat quietly down beside her, put my hands in my lap, and waited.

"Oh, you monster, you monster!" she said.

Chapter 134

Derry sat up hump-shouldered and weeping.

I reached to place my palm on her shoulder. She immediately pulled away as if stung.

"Derry?" I said. "I am a monster. But perhaps I can be your monster?"

"This is such a mess, I don't know what to do," she said sniffing.

"I can see it's nearly impossible for a person like you to accept me. I know," I said gravely.

"Bill, I called you a monster, but you haven't been. You've been the only thing I could trust to see what's going on around me. I know that. But it's so confusing. And the life of my child is at stake."

"I can help you see the world as it is, and believe it or not, it can get better. It is better." I felt very uneasy saying these words. Words that I could not believe, though I believed the world could be better for humans.

Chapter 135

Derry and I sat together at her kitchen table, having coffee, and letting Derry recover a bit from this last unveiling of bad news. Derry let me know that she'd have a long appointment in the afternoon the next day, and I'd need to wait in the lobby. I accepted this. Derry didn't mention her husband again that night. I didn't force her to any conclusions about what needed to be done.

Then my curiosity got to me. And I asked.

"Derry, what does your ESP tell you about me? Right now?"

Derry looked at me, but her eyes fell to the table top as quickly as a raindrop.

She shook her head, rose, and left the room.

I heard her bedroom door close.

Then I heard it lock.

Chapter 136

Derry's living room grew dark. I sat and thought about her. I thought of her sitting in her bedroom. I thought of her locked door. And I knew what it was like to be alone and locked in with a vampire at your door. And although I had Derry where I could use her, I knew too well what it was like for her, the anguish and feelings she must be experiencing.

I went to her door in the darkness.

"Derry," I called, "I won't do this. I won't put you in a world where you are a prisoner in your own bedroom. Hear me, Derry, I won't put you in a world where you are completely hemmed in by vampires. I won't be part of that. I just want you to know, you are not a prisoner, or a victim of this, you are free. You are free to do whatever you want, need, or decided to do."

"Derry, you need to understand that you are free."

I called this last message through the dark of the locked door. Then I returned and lay down on her couch.

Chapter 137

In the deep night, I was looking at the ceiling on Derry's couch when I realized there was another person in the room. The steps were quiet, guarded, and cautious. I shot out my senses into the dark to determine if there were danger. Someone was approaching, quietly coming near, a human. I waited as someone knelt at my shoulder.

When she whispered, her lips were so close I could feel her breath on my cheek. Her voice was calm. I could feel the slightest radiation of body heat, a flowery scent, a gentleness of motion that told me she was undressed.

"Bill, please, come with me," she said. She took my hand and stood, pulling me up from the couch. In the dark, I could just make out the gentle silhouette of her unclothed breasts and hips.

She walked me by the hand into her bedroom.

There across the bed's white sheets was a single streak of moonlight, an intensely white banner.

I could see her better now. She was incredibly beautiful. Naked and then urgent against me.

I kissed her. I laid her on the bed, the white banner flashing magnificently across her body, as I struggled to free myself of my monster's clothes.

I kissed her and was upon her.

"You won't make me a vampire, will you?" she gasped.

"No. Never, I would never do that," I whispered.

And then I felt her against me and my pleasure was great.

Chapter 138

The sexual act is so beautiful, lovely, short-lived. Breathless and spent, I was kissing Derry. Her mouth was closed in half-smile.

"I was afraid," said Derry.

"You asked me what my ESP told me." She opened her eyes to look at me hovering near. "I didn't tell you."

"And, what was that?" I asked.

"It told me we would be lovers."

"I understand," I said, "One more terrible thing to accept."

"No, sometimes, it's difficult to accept things that your senses tell you will be wonderful."

And there, with the great banner of love's moonlight across Derry's shoulder, chest, and abdomen, it was wonderful.

Chapter 139

Ah, vampire love, and human love, should never the two mix.

Chapter 140

The next day, Derry and I followed our routine of going to the Sunnyrock Home for Children. Nothing was said of the night's occasion. I simply noticed that Derry walked an inch or so closer to me as we crossed the park, she talking of the morning's duties, me remaining quiet. I didn't want to spoil things with talk of vampires.

It was getting pretty conspicuous that I was hanging around the Home. Certain children came up and greeted me hopefully each day. I sat outside Derry's office or in the lobby or walked the halls. I saw the boy Kelly in the hallway and said hello. He was extremely reluctant to greet me, as if I could be infected by his shame.

"How are you?" I asked.

"Okay, I guess," he said.

"You get over the other day in the park?" I asked.

He only shrugged.

"It wasn't your fault, you didn't know. You couldn't know, you know?"

"I know," he said.

I smiled. He laughed.

"Now we both know," I said.

"I know," smiled Kelly.

"No way," I said.

Kelly laughed again.

"Maybe we could go to the park again sometime?"

"Yeah!"

With that Kelly took his leave walking off with lighter steps.

It was then I looked down the hall and spotted Fred the Janitor. He was leaning on his mop, watching me with a frown and a blackness in his eyes that only my kindred can muster, one that puts a chill on icicles.

I smiled and nodded with a little wag from my cane.

Chapter 141

That afternoon Derry asked me to wait in the lobby as a married couple came to meet with her. I moved down to the reception area and waited. Hilda, the Busy, came up and offered me coffee, which I declined. It was strange how Hilda accepted my being there without much reflection. I guess her trust in Derry's judgment was deep enough thus.

But after several minutes, I got up and went to the edge of the hallway where Derry's office was. I stationed myself like a distant sentry watching her door. Just then at the other end of the hallway, Derry appeared hand in hand with a small girl hugging a doll. Derry was talking encouragement to her as they approached her office door and then entered.

A minute or two later, Derry reappeared, talking back through office door as she closed it. Once it was closed, Derry turned and walked hurriedly down the hall.

I followed her.

She turned at the next hall and went to a far door.

She unlocked it and then disappeared inside.

When I tried to open it, the infirmary door was locked.

Chapter 142

We had been sitting in silence at the kitchen table for several minutes, each lost in our thoughts. Then Derry straightened her shoulders.

"What's it like to be a vampire?"

I shook my head slowly at a hard question.

"It's a void, an emptiness. You don't really believe or feel anything of your own. It's a kind of black seeing. That's why vampires work so hard to gain the emotional blood of a human. To fill themselves with anything. Love, hate, disgust, anger, drunkenness, misery, remorse, the excitement of conquest, bloodlust, fury, vampires feed on any of these, and many more. Anything they can stir up. It is isolation, life at the bottom of the abyss, a long unending need."

Derry looked at me her face hard and solemn as a statue.

I tried to bring some humor into it.

"I even know a vampire who tried to feed off the pain of stubbed toes."

"Gosh," smiled Derry, shaking her head.

Chapter 143

Why do children's tears kill vampires so effectively?

I think it's because their bodies physically recognize that a child's tears represent all they have lost.

It's too much to bear.

They die like bugs in a vice.

Chapter 144

In the moonlight, with Derry pressed against me in her bed, she asked the most difficult question.

"Bill, how did you become a vampire? Were you born one?"

I held my breath. This was a tough story to tell.

"No. It takes a vampire to make a vampire. It's a disease that is passed from one to another."

I felt Derry's warmth against me, as I felt only cold in my chest, and I looked out the window into the blackness, not wanting to tell the story that had raised my eternal hate.

"How did you become one?" asked Derry solemnly.

"Long ago..." I said.

"When knight's were bold and armor shining...?" kidded Derry pressing closer to me as if I were beginning a children's story.

Derry didn't know it, but this was not far from the truth.

"Long ago when nights were cold and the moon shining," I said, "I lived in a small home with my wife and daughter. And one day a vampire came through my fields, and found my daughter playing. And he destroyed her. She was just eleven."

Derry's hand tightened on my shoulder.

"I found out later his name was Hierpat. He was a very old vampire."

I hesitated.

"And he is the same vampire that is after your son."

Chapter 145

"But what happened? How did you become a vampire?"

"It's painful to tell, and to hear, are you sure you want to know?"

"Yes." Derry's voice was resolute in the darkness.

"Well, one day, this vampire came through my fields, and he found my daughter. He caught her and led her away on a rope into the woods. I found her hands tied and the rope still around her neck. He had caught her and pulled her into the woods. And there he did the unimaginable, the unspeakable to a little girl."

I stopped. I could not speak further.

This horror sat with such stillness in the room Derry was afraid to move.

"I found her that evening, dirtied and dead, in the woods at the edge of my field."

I shook my head, "But Derry, this is no strange story, it happens all the time in this marvelous world of ours. We've always lived among such predators. This was just a time before we put children's faces on milk cartons and flimsy postcards. Vampires, vampires like this Hierpat have roamed for centuries. My daughter was not the only one, but only one of many, Derry."

"But how did that make you a vampire?" asked Derry.

"After this happened, my wife could not bear it. She lost herself when her daughter was so violated. There was no talking to her, there was no medicine, there was no mercy or understanding she could accept. She howled and tore her clothes, she wandered the woods and fields in rags, looking for Hierpat. She never found anything but the blackness within her, this abyss of loss. Then she hung herself. She hung herself with the same rope that had bound our daughter."

I grimaced.

"And you, Bill, what about you?"

"I didn't do so good, either," I shrugged.

I told Derry that for days I had sat alone in my home, unmoving, eating nothing. Eventually a neighbor found me and took me to his home. There he fed me his wine and bread. But within days I wandered away.

I didn't know it, but I was on the road to becoming a vampire.

Chapter 146

I found myself walking in a dark forest. It could have been days or months, I didn't know, for I had no sense of time. Darkened boughs hung over my head, low ground fog hugged my legs as I trod piney soil with mud soaked feet. Smoky banners of light shown here and there through the trees as if beacons were calling me this way or that, without goal, across the forest floor. I heard sudden caws, rustlings of escape in the bushes next to me; I merely looked in that direction. I was too numb to be startled. On occasion, I saw other figures, humans toiling in the distance, slowly digging, pulling up plants, chopping, eeking a living from the meager offerings of the forest's moss and

195

slime. But when I approached, these humans moved off quickly in suspicion and silence, looking over their shoulders as they retreated, tools up in hand like weapons as if I were an approaching beast.

I was bewildered and could only focus on myself, my deep and ravenous hunger.

I looked about me at the poisonous toadstools, the slugs, the spidery mosses and bitter Trilliums leaves, the spongy and spiny soil, the callous roots stiff and hard as animal bones, and there I found myself, my mouth watering with hunger. With no food in sight. I did not even know what I could eat.

I was alone in a forest without name. And so bewildered, I didn't know my own name.

Chapter 147

It was a forest landscape without compassion.

Chapter 148

"I was lost," I said to Derry through the darkness, "in a place where I fear many are lost."

Derry nodded gravely, her sympathy for my pain evident in the tightness of her arms clenched around my chest.

I felt her warm cheek press to my shoulder.

"I wish I could have found you," said Derry.

What a plain and beautiful heart she was.

"Go on, Bill, tell me all," she whispered.

"Someone, something did find me," I said ruefully.

Chapter 149

One night in the moonlight, dirty and tired, I came upon a black tarn, its water glassy and still. There beside it knelt a woman. She was slowly washing herself. She had raven black hair, long down her back. She was unbloused, squatting, washing her breasts with the black water. Half-dressed, a white diaphanous robe at her waist, her exposed shoulders and chest were pale under the bright moon, her breasts soft and moonlit.

They were so different from the world I had just come from. I slowly knelt and wept.

And a voice said, "My name is Tala. Get up. Come with me."

Chapter 150

In my suffering, I didn't know what to do, so I followed this voice, this calling woman with black hair. And she led me, dirty and disheveled, like an unconscious beast on a path only she saw.

As I walked behind her through the forest, she would turn and coax me forward. In the moonlight, her face was pale, her lips black, held in a crooked smile. She walked with an eerie grace. And each time she raised her hand to me, beckoning me forward in my misery, I could only whisper, "Please..."

We came to a small hut on the edge of a hillside, and there above the hill stood the black margin of a castle, silhouetted on the horizon by a money-silver moon draped with silver clouds with black faces.

"I live there," said the woman to me, "But you must rest here and sleep."

Her hand waved to the black door of the hut.

"There is food there. Go in," said the woman, "I will come back to see you."

"When you have rested and eaten, clean yourself for me, for my return."

Without a word, I nodded and entered the hut.

The door shut behind me.

It was then latched from the outside.

Chapter 151

Within the black hut, I fell upon a basket of bread and fruit. I ate wolfishly then fell asleep.

Chapter 152

The next morning when I woke bright swords of light were stabbed through the wooden slats of the windows and fastened door. The door was shut tight, didn't budge when I pressed against it. I looked out through the cracks to see a bright Spring, a green meadow peopled with a great mass of scarlet poppies, song birds singing, mists simmering from damp ground. I sensed the morning stones were warm as flesh. Spinning yellow and blue butterflies were making aimless, unconscious turns like the souls of flowers flying toward heaven. I looked out from the slats and could see Spring.

But I could not reach it.

I looked about the hut, its interior well furnished with wooden cupboards, stocked shelves, a larder of flour, salts, lard, beans, and even a basket of cakes. Across the wide room was a made bed, covered with clean sheepskins that I had not yet slept in. In my fatigue, in the darkness, I had slipped to the floor and slept on the planks. As I looked about, there was an earthen jug of water, a large ceramic basin, and soap. And upon a chair, clean clothes and even boots.

I ate again, but this time tasting my food. I washed and dressed.

And then waited for my mistress.

Chapter 153

It was late evening when I heard the jangle of heavy bells. I went to the door and strained to see out the cracks. A black horse approached with three iron bells upon its chest that clanked and lolled like tongues as it walked. Upon the horse was the woman who had found me.

I stared uneasily at this stunning woman.

She was dressed in white gown that lay over the horse's back like a blanket. Her face was a white oval, her black hair long and flowing down her back. And from her hips to her chest her body was tightly clasped in a white bodice that squeezed her belly and breasts fastened with a web of criss-crossed cords. In her hand was a worn crop which she lightly tapped to the horse's haunch. The horse stopped and swung its head toward the hut door as I watched. It chewed its bridal and pawed and the woman leaned forward and called.

"I'm here. Tala! The one who found you."

"I can't come out. The door is shut!" I called.

The woman gave a crooked smile with her purple lips and laughed.

"Of course it is," said Tala. "We don't want anyone coming around and finding you, do we?"

"Please, open the door," I called.

The woman dismounted easily. She pushed her riding crop beneath the saddle and the black horse walked unconcerned into the meadow.

Tala now stood before the door.

"Get back! While I open it," she commanded.

I stepped back a few steps and waited. I heard the outside latch lift and the door creak.

I stepped back again to allow the lady enter.

Chapter 154

When she turned from latching the door behind her she was already smiling at me.

"I'm Tala."

"Yes," I said. I nodded in a slight bow.

"And you, your name?" I could see she was amused by me. I felt like a shadow person standing before her.

"Guillaume. My name is Guillaume," I said.

"Thank you for washing at least. You look much better than when I found you."

"Thank you for letting me come here," I said. "I have nothing to repay you."

"Nothing?" said Tala chiding me. She touched her hand to the top of her neck, above the criss-cross cords of her bodice, in mock-dismay.

I shook my head.

"We'll see about that," she laughed. It was a deep laugh from her bowels. I was surprised by it.

"Can we go outside?" I asked.

"No. No one must see you. Especially my husband. You understand? We must stay in."

Tala looked at me, a warning glint filling her black eyes.

I nodded.

"You must stay here, within, until I say it is time to go. It isn't safe, otherwise. I give you this food, shelter, and clothing, but you must do what I say."

"Yes," I said.

"You have eaten?" she asked.

"Yes."

"You have washed and put on my clothes?"

"Yes," I said again.

"And so...?" she looked at me coaxing a response.

"Thank you," I said. "I had nothing. You helped me. I was a beast from the woods, but you weren't afraid and you helped me. Thank you. Thank you, Tala." I swallowed as I said this. I could barely look at her, her feminine image was so strong and oppressively intent on me.

"Yes, that's right," she said. "I have brought you back from that forest to be here. I'm glad you remember that. You should. You are mine now, so to speak!" Tala laughed.

"Agreed?" she said, chiding me.

202

"Agreed," I said.

"Oh good," Tala said, as if relieved and surprised.

"Why? Why did you help me? Most would have run away. Especially finding you as you were by the water."

"Half-dressed, yes, you did see things, didn't you?" Tala laughed.

I nodded.

"And it made you weep," continued Tala, "Why Guillaume, what a great compliment that is, to have a man kneel weeping before you. Weeping at the sight of me, bare and exposed."

I looked to the floor and back at Tala, uncomfortable and not seeing what she was implying.

"It made me feel quite, quite powerful. To find you, a blithering mess, kneeling before me. I felt I could do anything I wanted with you."

"Yes," I said in confession. I felt humiliation as if it were I who was half-naked.

"And so, Sweet Guillaume, I took you here and clothed and fed you. Why? Well, why do we feed our horses, poultry, and livestock? We must if we're to keep them. We must. And so you must be fed, too."

"I accept this, Tala," I said. "I will do whatever you want."

"But please, leave the door open," I said.

"No. My husband in the castle must never find you. You understand?" said Tala sternly. "You must stay within until you are ready and I know it is safe to let you out."

"I am your prisoner," I said with a grimace.

"Yes," said Tala amused. "Oh yes, that is why I want you. I want all of you."

And then she fell upon me in a great and fervid struggle to have me.

And I, I would have her as well. I pulled apart her white bodice and planted my mouth upon her breast.

Chapter 155

"Why did you agree?" interrupted Derry. "Food and clothing, they mean nothing. There's no binding force for having received them. You did not need to submit."

"There is only one answer," I replied, "Despair. Deep and unconscious despair."

Chapter 156

Derry squirmed uneasily next to me. I looked back over my shoulder but could not see her. It was probably for the best. This story was an ugly one to tell a lover.

"I was an animal for her," I said. "Each evening she left, locking me in. Each afternoon, she came back, now with more food, clothing. And always another dress that she made me tear from her chest. I must have her before I eat. And she taught me the ways in which it must be done."

"I spent weeks within the hut, waiting, always waiting her return. At first, I felt myself regaining my strength. But then after a prolonged period confined within the small enclosure, I felt myself fading again. I was becoming weaker without fresh air or exercise. At nights, Tala would mount me. I cooperated as I saw nothing but my own black world about me. Each night, before she left, she warned me of her husband in the castle. I must not leave for her safety. And I became weaker and weaker. Once again, I was losing myself as I'd lost myself in the forest. I was losing myself again to Tala, with her rabid sexual appetite, daily feeding upon my captive self. I realized Tala was now the forest I was lost in. And she would never let me leave."

I spoke these words into the blackness before me.

"You see, I didn't know that Tala was a vampire."

Chapter 157

I realize now how it had happened slowly. As I grew more house-bound and weak, Tala's desires seemed to kindle more. She came into the hut each evening relentlessly. Even when I was dozing and nearly lifeless upon the cot, I would find her naked astride me, tearing from me what satisfaction she could as she looked down in the fading animal below her. I was so tired, all I wanted was sleep, endless sleep. And there she was hovering above my face, her body grinding against me, her breasts waving loose, and the grimacing look of vampire consummation hardening her face. She would have every last ounce of me. In the darkness, I fell back. I felt her shiver and lift from above me. I saw her blackness, her being leave the hut, heard her laughter and last words to me, taking with her the last of myself.

I was empty. Consumed with self-loathing.

And then I saw the hut door was open.

Tala had left me.

Chapter 158

Confused, I wandered the farm roads, feeling only one thing: I was no longer a human being. I was something else. Putrid, weak, non-living. A ravishing hunger, devoid of caring what I fed upon. A rodent, insect, or slug, I could suck its life force from it without wanting or caring anything about it. I was just this side of the dead.

And I was walking.

It was days later when I realized I had desires that I could never bring into the light, not without bringing myself and others threat and great pain.

And I realized I was a vampire.

I couldn't walk in the light of day anymore, I had to walk in the night of my covert desires. And these needs went wherever I went.

Chapter 159

I coughed to clear my throat, then continued my story to Derry.

"Over time, I learned to move and walk and talk among the living. Cloaking my being enough to have other lives overlook my monsterdom stumbling among them. With vampire skill, I cloaked myself and my intentions, seemingly working, seemingly sharing in life with unsuspecting humans, when I was worse than a fox in the hen house—I was a black and snarling wolf in the hen house waiting for the farmer's egg-picking wife."

Derry was now utterly still behind me.

Chapter 160

And then I took victims myself in my confusion.

The confusion of a newly formed vampire.

I approached others, women who were susceptible to my attentions, women whose desires were unmet. Some young, some middle-aged. When they found me near them, I looked within their lives, saw the strains and stresses, and acknowledged their pain. I spoke of their pains back to them. I spoke with kindness and perception. I was always careful to hide my sharpest fangs behind my smile, metaphorically, of course. Vampire's don't need those Hollywood dog-fang teeth kids and adults wear at Halloween. Our victims offer us their blood. Offer their blood through their already open wounds. And to these women, I was irresistible.

To them, I seemed the way out, when I was actually on the way in.

And so I took these women, ravished them. They admired me for my brutish sexuality, my slow loving finesse, my warmth in approaching them from behind which aroused them, the calm of my voice, the confidence in my pulling them to my chest and kissing them until their brains melted. You see, as a vampire, I knew the secret gifts to offer. I could see the black needs hidden in their darkness, and offer black gifts for their delighted response. More than once I met shivering and urgent women, panting and climbing against me behind the woodshed, wearing nothing beneath their frilly nightgowns.

And I drank deep.

I felt this was the real life. The vampire life. Of course, I didn't want the women, I wanted their emotional blood. And the women thought I wanted them. But this was not so.

I would drink all of them and always leave them to their disappointment.

But all was not good for me. No.

After killing the spirits of another, drinking the love dry from the blood of my victim, knowing the ecstasy and temporary fulfillment, then later I also know the extreme isolation, the utter loneliness of being myself. And this utter loneliness and knowledge of death is the coffin I must lay back and sleep in.

Chapter 161

"I began to learn about vampires." I said to Derry, " I learned to understand our thinking, our emptiness. I found out that many are wanderers, aimless, homeless, even when they are rich and have homes. I found out that some vampires are racists focusing on children of a particular color. Others try farming, forming religious cults including whole families in an effort to create a steady supply of amenable victims, essentially raising cattle. Still others create vampire schools, stealing the spirits from the children: out come the walking dead, homogenized for the factories and offices of the dead. And suddenly there was a whole vampire culture to learn. A culture of black needs, ugliness, and unhappiness. A culture being passed down."

"For centuries."

Chapter 162

And I remembered the last thing Tala said to me before she went out the hut door, turning to me with her irresistible snaky smile:

"By the way, Guillaume, Hierpat is the one who sent me to you. He gave you to me as a gift. To bring you across."

"Who is Hierpat?" I asked, weak upon my bed.

Tala laughed, "He is my husband, the vampire that killed your wife and daughter."

Then she left the door open wide.

Chapter 163

I finished my story. Derry nudge me into sitting up on the bed.

"Bill, you have to go now. I'm going to be sick."

I got up and left her in the dim room.

Chapter 164

And so, I was a vampire.

And I could either end my life in a world I no longer wanted to be part of—

Or I could kill all those vampire motherfuckers.

The Pursuit

Derry's Vampire

Chapter 165

In the darkness I approached the back of the orphanage. Lights were on overhead in several windows here and there, I supposed where children were doing lonely homework. I was about to do a little lonely homework myself, a little janitorial work, so to speak.

I never skulk about buildings. I walk casually, self-assured, holding my cane under my arm. I mean to look more like an inspector than a monster stepping out of the alley shadows.

I walked to the back step, sentry posted by two overflowing garbage cans. Several cars of older vintage were parked in the back lot, their front windows fogging with the night moisture. It was only 10:00 o'clock but quite dark. Nothing was moving back here, much to my satisfaction. My cane under one arm, my holstered squirt gun under the other covered by my black leather jacket, I walked up to the back door and tried it.

It swung open with ease.

You could count on Fred the Janitor to leave the back door open for any old street monster.

Chapter 166

I walked slowly down the back hallway on gummy linoleum, scuffed and dull, the kind that feels like treading on bubbles as you walk. I passed the open door of a laundry room where big industrial dryers and washers were bumping and thumping. I saw twisted sheets and blankets piled on the floor and children's clothes in pillow cases with names waiting in long lines for their institutional machining.

At the end of the hall I found Fred's door. It was marked "JANITOR" in black letters that had dripped and run like dried blood.

A small seam of light was escaping under the door.

I knew he was in there.

I twisted the door handle softly, but found it locked.

So it was going to have to be gangbusters.

I stepped back, put my shoulder forward, and smashed the door open.

"Surprise!" I said to the startled occupant of the room.

Chapter 166

I'd caught Fred in his nest, sitting at a desk surrounded by a scatter of open magazines, over-read and crinkled, a few glasses and a dirty plate. A few odd photos fell to the floor as Fred the Janitor, startled, looked up at his broken door to find a stranger bursting through.

His mouth open in consternation and surprise, he swept several of the magazines off the desk onto the floor beside him, but he didn't get up. Fred's ape forehead and black eyebrows were pushed forward like a visor as he frowned. He was really looking at me to see who I was.

"What the fuck are you doing here?" said Fred, recognizing me. "Why'd you break that goddamned door? Can't you knock? Get out!"

I raised both hands out at my sides like a black angel in appeasement, but said nothing.

"What is this? Some kind of robbery?" said Fred trying to make some sense of it all.

I smiled and shook my head. Fred had still not stood up. Against the wall was an unmade bed where Fred slept, above it a calendar photo of a boy in swimsuit holding a surfboard.

I walked over to Fred's desk and looked over the magazines.

They were mainly glossy photos of kids being put through pornographic acts.

As I looked over the pile, Fred defensively pushed a few more off the desk, falling to the floor. I realized why Fred hadn't gotten up. He didn't have on any pants.

Ah, yes, Fred was a candidate for NAVBLA: the National Vampire Boy Love Association. He'd been licking his chops and reading his little magazines.

"That is ugly stuff there, Fred," I said nodding at his desktop.

"You don't like it, get out!" spat Fred. He puffed up to make a good bluff.

It was all I could do to keep from laughing. I was so happy with the way things were going.

Chapter 167

I placed my cane down on the desk. Fred looked down at it, seeing the silver tip pointed directly at his chest and my hand at ready on the handle.

"What are you doing?" he exclaimed, getting the idea something dangerous was about to happen.

I rammed the cane all the way through his chest and into the back of the chair. I let Fred hold my cane as he gasped, attempting with a wobbly stumble to stand up.

I pulled my squirt gun from my holster, doffed the piece of duct tape, and squirted a clean dose into Fred's open mouth.

"Aghhh!" gargled Fred.

Fred was taken by wracking shivers. His eyes bulged like somebody run over by a steamroller, his face went purple, then he collapsed in spasms onto the pile of his dirty magazines.

"I don't like you, Fred," I said, "Get the point?"

Chapter 168

I think J. Edgar Hoover was one of America's most notorious vampires, preying on a hearty diet of criminals and politicians alike.

Chapter 169

Not all vampires are old evil men, as you might think. For example, there was Zelda, a sixteen-year-old runaway vampire girl who was taken in by a loving retired couple, Ed and Nel.

This couple, both in their seventies, drove by a street corner one day in their old clunker. There stood a disheveled adolescent, in striped tank top, jeans with holes in the knees, pulling at her stringy hair and looking around bewilderedly. She had a thumb out, but wasn't hitchhiking. This young vampire was trolling.

Ed and Nel saw Zelda, felt sorry, and decided to pull over. Zelda reminded them of their daughter at sixteen, who had later died in mid-life of cancer, bald and suffering, in a cancer ward ten years earlier.

"Can we help you, young lady?" called Ned from the lowered car window.

They sure could. Zelda pulled back her hair and saw caring surrogate parents (unlike her vampire relatives) and saw paradise. She took a ride with them home, had lunch, had dinner, had a nice night's sleep, and stayed for months.

Ed and Nel's faces began glowing. This little vampire was filling up their house.

During the six months Zelda stayed, Zelda stole a car, sold Ed's prize shotgun, poisoned the cat with slug bait (Zelda didn't like cats), caught gonorrhea behind the local tavern and then gave it to the 14-year-old boy next door, crashed the clunker, slugged a girl and gave her a black eye when Ed and Nel enrolled Zelda in high school, made a pass at Ed which nearly killed the old guy with embarrassment, and generally had a good time.

After each crisis, Ed would speak sternly, trying to straighten the girl out, but his heart wasn't in it. (He was already giving out.)

Nel would enter the girl's bedroom at night, whisper endearments, and stroke the vampire's forehead to soothe her.

Both were waking up more and more weary each day.

But Zelda the vampire just kept on piling up the woes, until Ed and Nel were just dragging themselves around like zombies, their eyes dead.

Of course, Zelda didn't know why she was handing out all that punishment. Personal history issues, naturally.

It's just Ed and Nel had invited a vampire into their house.

And that's what vampire do, drain you of everything they can.

Zelda was getting fat and sassy. One happy little piggy vampire.

Ed's heart finally failed. Zelda attended the funeral in black mini-skirt with fist-size holes in her nylons, such that even the priest was taking second looks at her. Nel succumbed two weeks later of grief and weariness facing alone the omniverous young Zelda.

So, of course, Zelda inherits all Ed and Nel's stuff.

As a confirmed vampire, Zelda couldn't ever see anyone else, just her desires.

So she was quite surprised when I entered her bedroom one night and staked her to the wall, right through the heart, and fed her my potion, the secret vampire sauce that killed her.

I'd heard about Zelda by sneaking into a church and taking Ed's confession when he told the whole story, crying with hopelessness, a few weeks before he died.

Sneaking into a confessional and hearing stories is a good way to find out about vampires and victims. You should try it sometime.

Chapter 170

I knocked on Derry's office door and she looked up from her phone conversation and waved me in.

I sat quietly on the black chair before her desk.

"Well, you'll just have to get Fred to fix it," said Derry. She eyed me and nodded to let me know the conversation would end in a moment.

"Well, Fred will be in shortly I expect," said Derry. Then she said bye and hung up.

"Hi, how are you?" said Derry to me. She leaned forward, looking like she wanted to reach across the desk, but not daring to.

"Fine," I said.

"Why did you come in?" asked Derry.

"I wanted to talk with you a bit," I said.

"You look so serious," said Derry.

I nodded without reply.

"Well, spit it out," she said with a cordial nod. "Is it something about the kids here? About me?"

"No," I said. "It's about vampires."

Derry's face whitened.

"Okay," she said evenly.

She waited for me to go on.

"Derry, there's a vampire living in this building."

"What?"

"Fred," I continued, "the Janitor, he's a vampire. I need to do something about him. You can't have him here."

"How do you know this? Are you sure?"

"I am," I said.

"I'll fire him now," said Derry.

I shook my head.

"Derry, we need to do something else more drastic."

"Like what?"

I merely looked at her.

She looked back realizing I was implying a dark act.

She shook her head, "No, no way."

"Derry, it's up to you, you can fire him, and he moves on to other victims, or I can rid him from this earth."

I knew Derry would never consent to murder.

"Derry, it is what I do, why I'm here," I insisted.

Derry sat back and looked at me. It was a long pause.

"You've already killed him," she said with widening eyes.

Her psychic abilities were infallible.

"Yes," I said. Her face was melting with emotion.

Then I put back my head and laughed.

Derry continued to look at me astounded.

"You killed my janitor," said Derry incredulous.

I stopped laughing.

"Excuse me, Derry, laughter is the one pleasure I get from this."

I gave her a sheepish smile. I shrugged.

"The rest is only cold and emptiness," I said.

Chapter 171

Vampires are masters at dealing pain. They can be subtle and atrociously accurate.

Take for example little Gwen Grant and her 3rd grade vampire teacher out of Huston Texas. This stodgy vampire assigned her class, mainly lower income kids from houses missing shingles, to bring newspapers to cover their desks for an art project the next day. If they didn't bring in the newspapers, they couldn't do the project.

Little Gwen Grant, a good-hearted cherub, knew most of the kids wouldn't bring newspapers. Newspapers weren't likely to be found in many of the houses where black-and-white TV was the main form of reading.

So the next morning she gathered an armload of extra newspapers from her home to bring in for the other kids. She showed the teacher her good-hearted gift so that everyone could do the project.

The vampire response: "These people have to learn to take care of themselves. Take those newspapers down to the furnace and burn them!"

The vampire response: burn the gift right in front of the giver.

Boy, if I ever catch that old vampire, I'm giving her a double squirt.

Chapter 172

The little plastic box on the side of Derry's desk crackled into life.

Hilda's voice came though, roughened by electronic scuffing.

"Derry, Derry, sorry to interrupt."

"What is it, Hilda?" asked Derry putting a finger on the box and leaning toward it.

"Your husband's here. He arrived and said he had a meeting with you. But he wouldn't wait for me to call you. He just walked off the down the hall."

Derry looked at me.

"Let's go," I said.

I got up behind Derry as she rushed toward her door. When she opened it and went out, I expected her to turn left toward the infirmary. But she went right toward the dorm rooms.

She began jogging down the hall, me just a step or two behind. We dashed up a flight of stairs.

When we entered the second floor hallway, there was Derry's husband at the far end. He was quickly walking from door and door, pulling them open and looking in.

"Chuck!," shouted Derry sternly.

This single shout conveyed the meaning "Stop!", "What are you doing here?," and with a little "You bastard" thrown in as well.

Derry's husband turned to look our way, sneering, "You know what I'm here for..." then he stopped in mid-sentence. He'd spotted me behind Derry.

His mouth closed as we stared at each other. Derry looked over at me.

Then he ran.

In an instant, I was after him. I felt my vampire heart rise for the chase. I was gripping my cane by the middle grip, raising it up and down like a frantic marching band leader as I dashed toward the fleeing vampire, who'd just made the stairwell. His first leap, he must have descended five stairs.

"Bill!" I heard Derry call behind me. I ignored Derry's plea and charged to catch up.

I jumped the entire first flight, and then the second. When I hit the first floor, I was nearly on him.

But just then, looking back at me, he bowled through a group of five or six children, sending them sprawling in all directions. I had to slow and pick my way through the tangle so I wouldn't trample any arms or legs.

Derry's husband, chest pumping, made it to the front door.

And there was Derry, running down the far stairwell near him. Her arms were out, but they were pointed at me.

Derry's husband ducked out the door and headed running across the parking lot. He was headed toward the park. I liked the idea of that.

I ran up to Derry and passed her going out the orphanage door. As my feet hit the concrete, I figured I could catch him in a bout a half block.

"Stop! Bill, Stop!" I heard shouted behind me.

I slowed my pursuit to a trot, then stopped. Something in the urgency of Derry's call had quelled my blood-lust.

Derry's husband was running full tilt across the park muddy grass flying up behind him.

Boy, for a real estate agent, he could really cover a lot of property.

I returned to Derry, giving her a questioning look.

She shook her head angrily.

"You've already killed my janitor, I don't want you to kill my husband."

For Derry, I could see the great pain in this statement.

For me, I saw the underlying humor of it as well.

Chapter 173

That night as I sat with Derry at her kitchen table, I knew the clock was ticking. One of Heirpat's vampires had edged into the school. And from Derry's morose face, I could tell it was not good that it had been Derry's ex-husband. She had little to say. Perhaps she intuited that I did, that I needed to explain the next steps for us.

"Derry, I need to pursue your husband."

Derry's eyes widened and she sat back.

"What do you mean *pursue*?"

"I need to pursue what he knows. Another vampire brought him across."

"His new little real estate receptionist," muttered Derry.

"Likely," I said. "And that vampire is in contact with Heirpat. It is our one main lead. I need to pursue it, otherwise we're simply waiting for big surprises that we may not be able to handle."

Derry nodded.

Something had changed about Derry. She was calm, she wasn't in denial, she was going now with her intuition and what she knew. It must have been hard for her to let go and fly by the seat of her pants. But she was going with it, determined, going on no matter what came. And I felt I had a partner now.

"Will you...?" asked Derry. She looked away. "I don't want you to. I loved him once."

"Love dies hard. Some people might welcome an avenging vampire falling on the head of an ex-lover."

"Not me," said Derry.

I nodded in my turn. I didn't go into it further. The inevitable had to happen and always did. And the inevitable was me.

"Love is a problem, if you believe in it," I said.

"And you don't?" asked Derry.

"I can't," I said.

Derry looked at me with the bags of a woman's pity in her eyes.

"Why don't you believe in love?"

"Because when love fails, we remain the keepers of the children," I said.

"And even that has been denied me."

Chapter 174

The telephone ring crisped the air. Both Derry and I looked askance at each other as it rang several times.

I walked over and answered it.

"Hello?" I said.

"*Bonjour mon maudit cousin, ca va?*" said the raspy voice.

"*Qu'est que tu vuex?*" I said.

"*Rendez-vous a 1050 Connecticut. En duexs heurs. Soyez tout seul.*"

"*Bien,*" I said and put down the receiver.

"Who was that?" asked Derry, alarm entering her voice. I think my speaking French had thrown her.

"Heirpat," I said. "He wants to meet. 1050 Connecticut."

"That's down in the industrial section. Why there? What does he want?"

"What does a vampire ever want?" I shrugged. "I've got to be there in two hours."

"It's a trap, you know that. What else could it be?"

"A trap only works if you don't know about it," I said. "I must go."

"I don't want you to. We should do this on our terms."

"Our terms up to now have been waiting. This could be the end of our quest. This might allow me to finish all this for me, you, and your son," I said firmly. I went and picked up my shoulder holster with its orange squirt gun. I checked it gingerly for leaks, then put it on. Then my black leather jacket.

Derry stood frowning the whole time.

Before I left, I turned back to Derry. "Derry, take this." I threw her my car keys. "If there's someone at the orphanage that is important to you, this might be a good time to take them on a long car ride, for several hours. And make sure no one can follow you."

Derry looked down at the keys in her hands and nodded.

"Where is your car?"

"It's a yellow Volvo station wagon, you'll find it parked on Balboa, a few blocks from here."

"Vampires drive the family station wagon?" asked Derry mustering a small smile.

"Right," I said.

I didn't say it was good for hauling bodies.

Chapter 175

Just as I was stepping out the door, Derry called for me to stop.

She came up and looked intently at me.

"Bill, listen to me," she said.

"Yes?"

"If someone tells you to look at something, don't look. Duck."

I looked at Derry's face, written deeply with urgency, and I knew this was a message from her ESP, and I knew not to question her.

I nodded and left.

Chapter 176

It was a longish walk over to the industrial section, the backyard of the City. I walked carefully alert to the surroundings. Huge warehouses, the kind with wooden walls and broken boards patched with rusty corrugated metal, stood like beached shipwrecks. Train tracks lay along the sides of the street like rusted exposed veins. Grass grew up out of the sidewalks. I walked steadily with my cane, looking left and right for ambush. I saw no one in the area. No cars moving. No one loading trucks. No bums drinking from bags on the back steps of the deserted truck docks.

Only a few black birds on the telephone wires watched mutely.

Although I expected to see more than one vampire, I hadn't brought the Big Squirt 2000. Only my little organge job, safely hidden beneath my coat. If Heirpat needed to surprise me, I also needed to surprise him.

I turned a corner on Connecticut and saw my destination. It was a large wooden structure with a swayback roof, the size of a football field. I walked entirely around it. Although there were small windows the size of bird houses around the upper eves, there were no openings at street level, except for a steel garage door, draped with chains, on one side of the building.

So that was the way I was supposed to enter.

I reached down and lifted and the door swung up with rusty screeches and the rattle of chains. The interior of the warehouse was dim as I stepped in.

There, like a huge inner-house within a house, stood a large concrete building. It was standing centered and alone within the dilapidated warehouse. The structure was painted white, with a single door in the end, reminding me of an over-sized military bunker. Except for barrels and a few pieces of broken down equipment lining the walls, the warehouse was empty but for this inner structure.

I walked to the bunker door and pushed it open gingerly with the head of my cane.

A light was on in the inner chamber. I walked in to find what seemed an empty office with several desks, chairs, and filing cabinets set about the room. All the desktops were empty of paper and dust on the chair seats.

And there, against the far wall was a great vault door. The kind of monstrous steel door your see with heavy wheels and hinges in banks who need to display some air of security. I went over to the door, tried to slide it back to see what was inside, but it held fast. Not a rattle or the slightest jimmy when I pulled on it full strength.

"Ah, I see you've found my little piggy bank," said a raspy voice behind me.

Chapter 177

I turned round to see an old man with a red bump on his forehead standing in the doorway. He was the same old man I'd conked in the park. Except now he was leering at me with the complete menacing power of an aged vampire. These looks were never deceiving.

"*C'est toi, alors*," grumbled the old vampire.

"*Et toi*," I said.

The old vampire was seeming to grow in size as I looked. He was puffing to fill the entire door case. Vampires in conflict make such displays. Something like puffer fish.

"I'm Heirpat," said the old man.

I realized I'd had this old bastard against a tree where I could have staked him, but didn't.

The old vampire laughed at my chagrin, his grizzled chin and extremely white teeth pointing at the ceiling. He looked now like an evil scull head on an athlete's body.

"Yes, you had me, young vampire, but your sense of propriety stopped you. Fool that you are. And you?"

"Guillaume Molliere," I said.

"We've met before, I take it?" asked the old man.

I began edging his way, my cane down at my side.

The old vampire's eyes went up. He put out a hand, first to motion me to stop, then a quick flick behind him, which brought into view three more lumbering vampires, whose dark faces and huge shoulders made them look like Huns in football gear. They stood at ready outside the room behind the old vampire's back.

"No closer," smiled Heirpat.

I stopped.

"I'll kill you or die trying," I said.

"Interesting," smiled the old man, he looked back at his little horde as if to share a joke.

"But I didn't bring you here to *kill you*," said Heirpat. His voice was lilting and free. He was getting a kick out of this.

"Why are you protecting this boy, why are you involved?" he asked.

"Why are you after him?" I returned.

"Oh, he represents danger to my realm. As you know, the vampire that feeds upon this one dies. We can't have that, can we?"

232

"After all your victims, what's one vampire more or less?" I shrugged. "I've lost count I've killed. You haven't been after me."

"Oh, well, I've just never noticed you before, Gui," said Heirpat.

"Perhaps you have," I said.

"Oh?" said Heirpat. He raised his eyebrows for me to go on.

I stood silent. I wasn't doing anything for him.

"So, I haven't come here to fight with you. Oh, the world and our many victims, they are so bountiful, there is plenty for you and me. I want to offer you whatever you want. Simply to desist. Simply to remove a small obstacle from my path. If I can give you what you want, our paths are the same."

"You can offer me only one thing," I said darkly.

Taking my deadly meaning instantly, Heirpat laughed hard. The room actually filled with his laughter and I grimaced to be surround by it. One of Heirpat's Hun vampires stepped into the room in front of him and stared malevolently. Heirpat put out a hand to hold the vampire soldier at rest.

"Well, I do have something to offer you. Here." Heirpat raised a hand and pressed on what looked like a garage door opener.

Behind me I heard a rumbling.

I turned my head to see the great vault door opening. Tons of steel were painfully pulling back. And revealed there was a great mass, a glittering spectacle of incredible porportions. A room the size of a bus station completely filled with cash, gelt galore, real moolaa. I saw a hundred heaps higher than a man's head. Actually just piles of treasure, gold bars, coins, jewelery, gold chalices, paper currency all strewn about in a great rubbish pile, confused and without order. All heaped in steep mounds that would require you to crawl up on your knees. It looked like the wealth of the entire world, poured into the vault from the back of dump trucks.

"A little something for you, please take it. Just relent a little bit," said Heirpat.

I sighed and shook my head. "How did you get all that?" I asked. I pointed the laughing head of my doggy cane back over my shoulder into the vault. I was watching Heirpat closely now.

"Oh, I've taken things from a few victims over the years," said Heirpat. Then he sneered, "And after the first million victims, pograms and such, it begins to add up."

Then Heirpat laughed again his terrible chilling laugh.

"Why? Why prey upon humans so?" I waved my arm behind me at the great vault of gold.

Heirpat's unrelenting eyes never left me.

"It is simply survival." Then the old bastard laughed, long and chillingly.

"Survival gone mad!" I said.

Chapter 178

"So, tell me, cousin, what do you want? Since I practically own the world, I can likely give it to you. We can have done with all this," coaxed Heirpat.

Beware the coaxing vampire.

I squeezed the grip of my trusty cane just the slightest.

That was all the answer Heirpat needed. He shook his head.

"Well, Gui, then why? Why would you refuse everything that stands behind you?" Heirpat trained his yellow eyes deeply into mine.

"I learned of you way back. Long ago. You killed my wife and daughter."

"Ah," said Heirpat with a confirming nod of the head, "so it's personal."

Heirpat looked left and nodded at the three vampires near him. They backed slowly out of sight.

"You know, cousin, there might be something from your daughter back there in my vault! Why don't you look?"

Irresistibly, I felt my head turning to look into Heirpat's vast vault of richess. Something from my daughter?

Then I remembered Derry's warning to me. And I hit the floor.

Chapter 179

The concussion of the blast was as if someone had slapped both my ears. A terrible impact and clang spat just feet above my head.

Sparks showered in an umbrella down on me.

I looked up to see a steel harpoon sticking out of the concrete wall.

I rose. Heirpat was lowering an oversize weapon with huge barrel, a modern day whaler's gun. His eyes were intensely angry. I supposed because he'd missed. He dropped the weapon with distaste.

"*A prochain fois!*" he growled, and then disappeared from the doorway. The heavy metal door rolled shut with a metallic clack.

I got up and walked over to the door to find it was locked fast. I cast a glance down at Heirpat's discarded harpoon gun.

I'll say one thing: I had to admire his choice of weapons.

Chapter 180

It took me roughly about six hours to break out. I just chipped away at the wall with the Heirpat's harpoon. The concrete was poor quality and broke into minute shards. It was hard work, but I kept slogging at it.

At the point when I first broke through with a fist size hole, I saw another face look back at me from the other side. It was the same vampire soldier that had entered the vault beside Heirpat.

When I saw him peering in like a man through an over-sized keyhole, I took out my squirt gun, pulled the tape, and squirted him right in the snout.

He grabbed his face with a gratifying scream and stepped back.

I stuck my arm through the hole and squirted in all directions.

More screams. More flailing about.

When I finally broke out, stepping through the concrete hole and looking around, there were three dead vampires, Heirpat's late guards, laying on the ground, arms over their heads, like victims of a miniature Pompeii.

No one else was about.

Before I left, I went around the warehouse setting different corners on fire. As I walked away, black smoke was already snaking from the windows.

I had walked halfway back to Derry's amid the banchee calls of sirens when the explosions began.

I looked back to see a skyscaper of flames and smoke rising. And there a huge black smoke ring from an explosion spinning.

Heirpat must have wired it for self-destruction.

Chapter 181

I found my yellow Volvo in the orphanage parking lot. It was 11:00 o'clock and quite dark. Derry's apartment had been empty. I was relieved to see the vehicle on familiar grounds.

The Orphanage front door was locked. No lights were on in the overhead dormitory rooms. But I saw one light on at the far end of the building, on the second floor, the infirmary side.

I went round the back and found the door still unlocked.

As I walked quietly down the hall to the infirmary, I saw the door wasn't shut properly. I pulled it open slowly and looked in.

The room was small, enough for six beds. The beds were empty except the far one, where Derry sat. A nurse in full white uniform looked up from an easy chair as I entered. She stood quickly, putting down a magazine and frowning.

"It's okay, Nelda," called Derry. "He's a friend."

Mounted high in the back corner of the room, so all the beds could see, a TV's gray face was shining down dully.

"Bill? What are you doing here?" called a voice under the TV.

I looked and saw Kelly sitting cross-legged under the set.

I walked up to Derry seated on the bed holding another boy. He was sick, with darken eyes and blank stare. Derry was stroking his forehead. I saw he was Kelly's identical twin.

And then I understood a little more.

238

Chapter 182

The TV was turned to the news. A column of smoke was rising behind firefighters and a man with a microphone.

Derry gave me a searching look.

"There was a big fire on Connecticut," she said.

"I know," I said.

"They found three bodies."

I nodded.

Derry looked down at her son, saying, "Johnny, this is Bill. He's helping us get you better."

The boy, deep in misery and depression, the helplessness of a new vampire, barely moved his eyes to me and back.

"Boy, look at the flames!" said Kelly to the TV screen.

"Did you....?" asked Derry.

"No," I said.

Chapter 183

Both Derry and I stood in silence a moment, temporarily stymied by disappointment.

"We went for a trip today, Bill!" called Kelly with a five-year-old's enthusiasm for the extraordinary. "All the way to China."

"China Camp, we went to China Camp," correct Derry.

"Have fun?" I asked Kelly.

"Yeah." Then he turned back to the gray TV.

"So what's next?" Derry said finally.

"You have two sons. Not one," I said.

"Yes," admitted Derry.

"And only one was attacked," I said. I understood now the real meaning of the close call with Kelly in the park.

"Let's talk about this later. Now, first things first," I said.

"What's that?" Derry asked.

"Let's go home."

Chapter 184

Kelly protested, "No, don't go, Mom. I don't want you to!" His face wrinkled into anger and desperation.

"You're going home, too," I said to Kelly. "You're coming home with your Mom. No more staying here at night."

"But," sputtered Derry.

"All right!" shouted Kelly. He got up and slammed into his Mother's side on the bed, clinging to her shoulder. The boy in Derry's arms blinked and frowned, then put his cheek closer to Derry's arm.

"He must be with us, now. It's no good here." I'd almost said too dangerous.

"Home!" said Kelly, pressing to his mother's shoulder.

"Are we taking Johnny, too? He's so sick," said Derry, "He need's Nelda's attention."

"No, he should stay here. He's safer here, away from us," I said.

I didn't say he wasn't in any immediate danger at all.

Once you're a vampire, other vampires lose interest.

Chapter 185

Derry knelt by the bed for several minutes taking leave of her sick son. Her face was nearly pressed to his ear talking.

Kelly and I were standing at the door, as was the nurse, with nothing to do. Kelly asked me if I was coming home, too.

"I'll be there for awhile," I said.

"Great! Can I play with your cane?" asked the boy.

"Maybe not just now," I said.

Finally Derry walked over to us. Her eyes were wet, but she smiled at Kelly as we turned to the door.

"Thanks, Nelda," called Derry over her shoulder as we exit.

"Bye," called Nelda, walking toward the boy's sick bed. She had a magazine in her hand as she walked.

Chapter 186

When we entered Derry's apartment we suddenly had a little fireball of elation running about. He went first to his room to check his toys, caromed about the apartment like a ricocheting beach ball, went into Derry's room for some high bounces on the bed, then came back and grabbed his mother by the thigh, planting his head against her.

Derry laughed.

"Home," he said.

Both Derry and I laughed.

Derry took Kelly off to his room to read him a book before he slept. I told Derry I'd make some hot chocolate and toast. While in the kitchen, I made some coffee as well.

I delivered my little repas, then left Derry and Kelly reading in bed, Kelly under his mother's arm, looking sleepy and fulfilled as Derry read an old fairytale.

I repaired to the kitchen to drink coffee and wait alone.

After a half-hour Derry appeared and shared coffee with me.

I told her of my little fiasco with Heirpat and narrow escape from a harpoon.

"Thanks," I said.

Derry nodded her head.

"I may know now why they're after your sons."

"Why," asked Derry, narrowing her eyes on me.

"Because they're twins, they share the same blood. If one can cure a vampire, then the other can as well."

"But Johnny's sick, he isn't cured," said Derry.

"No, but he can be. His blood cured the old vampire that died attacking him."

"But he became ill," injected Derry.

"But Kelly isn't," I said.

"I don't follow."

"Kelly could cure him," I said. "They can cure each other. They need only share a bit of their blood with the other."

"It wouldn't kill Johnny?" asked Derry.

"No, the vampire dies, the person returns," I said, "He's only five, not five hundred. He would be fine."

"How?"

"Whatever thing is in their blood does it," I said evasively.

"Well, let's do it now. Let's go cure my child!" said Derry with some exasperation.

I shook my head.

"Heirpat is not after him. He is after Kelly. If we cured him now, he would be in danger. We should not cure him until this is done. He's in no danger now."

"No!" said Derry, "He's sick. He's suffering. His misery is great. You saw it. We must do it now."

"No, Derry," I said firmly, "Life as a vampire is better than no life at all."

Derry looked at me, realizing that Heirpat was not out to convert Kelly to vampirehood, he was simply out to kill him.

Derry's face was glacial staring at me, near hate in her eyes.

That's all right, you can't kill this messenger.

"Well, I should be going," I said getting up.

"You're not staying here?"

"No," I said. "I'll be outside."

"Why?" asked Derry.

"Because you can't keep a vampire in the family," I said.

I rose and Derry walked me to her door.

Chapter 187

"Goodnight," I said. I was halfway out the door when Derry spoke up.

"Bill?"

"Yes?"

"You risked your life for me and my family today. Thank you."

"No pity for the loveless," I smiled, with a shake of my cane, "My motto."

Derry and I took an instant to look at each other.

"Why do you deny love?" asked Derry.

"It's like horses: if you need togetherness and love, you can be enslaved by it."

It sounded good, but it didn't ring true.

"You have to serve something," said Derry.

I looked at her, devoutly serving the children of her orphanage, creating a home and living space out of a brick environment. To what efforts she would go to serve the lost children.

I was beginning to feel like one of her lost children.

I'm afraid this could not be. I had lost my childhood and thus humanity long ago.

"I serve something," I said, "It's just I serve it up on a stick."

Derry laughed.

At least she could read my black humor.

Chapter 188

That night was an empty one for me. I moved with care around the building walkways, watching, walking quietly carrying my cane, not letting it tick the ground. There was a brisk wind that lifted the hair from my forehead, but which never penetrated the thick leather of my coat. Not that there was anything that could get chilled within me.

I remained in shadows, watching, watching throughout the night.

I saw no signs of predators or vampires. I saw no signs of watcher's eyes upon our camp.

As the night sky finally lightened, in the coldest hour just before dawn, I walked quickly to my apartment for something.

I returned, went up into Derry's building, and laid a black rose at her doorstep. So she would know that I had been there.

Chapter 189

I once knew a college student, John Tallman. I lived across the hall from him in an apartment house not far from the university. He was a electrical engineering student studying for his degree. He was a big grinning kid, played a bit of football in high school. We went to a few bars together. He didn't mind my black side or my poetry. He had a high school girlfriend name Janna.

Janna lived several hundred miles away in small town with her poor family. Her house was a shack. John had left to go get his degree, but took frequent trips back to see Janna. She was his small town girlfriend. She was also a vampire.

So while she waited for John's visits, John suspected she secretly fooled around with other guys.

I remember it was semester break and John received the letter. Janna was pregnant with John's baby. I realized he wasn't so sure.

John did a lot of sitting still, staring at the wall, thinking.

John and Janna got married and moved into his apartment. It was a big burden for John, getting married, finding a job, and keeping his studies going. Janna was happy as a little vampire-lark in her new apartment.

I moved on. A year later, John called and invited me to a party. I came to the apartment and drank wine with a small group of John's engineering buddies. The baby was in a little bed in the single bedroom. It was a cute baby, and not a vampire. (None are.) I remember Janna was happy on the couch talking to one of John's friends. A Bob Somebody. They were both holding wine glasses and talking. Later they walked down to the corner liquor store to get more wine.

"He's walking with my wife!" John said to me when he realized they'd gone.

I didn't say a word. I knew Janna was a vampire. I knew.

Two weeks later, I bought a pizza and dropped in by surprise at John's apartment. When I knocked on the door, Janna opened it.

I said hello to Janna. Then I looked in to see Bob Somebody sitting on the couch. He's holding a wine glass. There's another wine glass on the end table.

I played stupid.

I said, "Hi, I brought a pizza, where's John?"

"He's in class till nine," said Janna smiling cordial and inviting. Bob Somebody raised his wine glass, an unenthusiastic hi.

I handed Janna the pizza and said I'd come back another time.

I could hear the baby crying in the other room.

I should have gone back that night and did my thing. I should have staked her to her bed.

But I didn't. It would only have been more of a burden for John, with his new baby, though I knew no good would ever come of it.

So see, I let at least one vampire off.

Chapter 190

There is a rough nail that sticks out of the wall of my past. And it jabs into me deeply every time I pass.

It's the fact that I didn't help my family before their demise.

Chapter 191

The next morning I saw Derry and Kelly crossing the park. Kelly started running my way, but Derry called him back. I followed them to the Home. I waited outside the Home all day, watching. I met them crossing the park again and followed them home. They entered Derry's apartment building and disappeared. We exchanged nary a word that day.

Chapter 192

That night it rained. I stood wet in the alley, body tight as a pinecone. Large drops were falling hard from the eves making bullet holes and crowns in puddles. I had my cane clutched under my arm. I was swaying from foot to foot like elephants do. Like them, I didn't expect my chains to be released in the darkness. Then I heard footsteps in a nearby stairwell.

Someone was standing there, leaning, looking round. Her coat was tight, her collar up, but she wore no hat.

Finally she saw me. She stepped my way.

"Bill, come back in. Please."

She didn't bother to call again, she simply turned and began climbing the stairwell into the building.

I followed her in my turn.

On entering her apartment, I saw only the kitchen light was on. I went in to find Derry seated at the table, a cup of coffee already poured for me, black and steaming. I took off my wet jacket and laid it on the back of the chair.

I sat down and looked at Derry once. Then we drank our coffee in silence.

Chapter 193

"You set such store in love," I said.

Derry shrugged, "I suppose so. But you have to work from a good foundation. You can't change evolutionary trends or eliminate suffering. You have to accept the world as it is to make a difference. But if you work from love, your mistakes and your karma will not travel far. What other gift of substance, real change can you offer the world?"

"Vengence and death," I said, the perfect little vampire.

I watched the lovely blue of Derry's eyes wilt a bit.

"There's no change there," said Derry dead calm.

"Ask the dead if it changed their lives," I said.

Derry sniffed.

"We're all dead anyway, why rush history?"

I looked at Derry stonily.

"Wouldn't you like to stick around with me a little longer?" she said.

"Yes," I admitted.

I looked at Derry's kind and pleading face. She had me.

"Then let's go to bed. What do you say to that, Mr. Vampire?"

"When invited into love's bed, never tarry."

Eternal vampire wisdom written by yours truly that.

Chapter 194

The next morning at breakfast, Kelly was only a little surprised to see me at the kitchen table. He was still young enough to say hi and accept the adult world without a second thought, sitting down to cereal and sliced peaches.

I sat there and watched him eat like a professional. Derry called advice as she busied a bit about the kitchen, made lunches, and explained the day's routine to Kelly.

At one point, Derry helped him tie his shoes. The strings had been flapping like beagle ears.

"There you go," she said smiling, "all tied up."

Kelly threw his arms around his Mother's neck to stop her from rising.

Derry laughed.

Chapter 195

We went to the Home. I saw noone watching us from the park. As Derry worked, Kelly played with orphanage friends, on the playground, in the halls, in and out of the rooms. I stuck close, cane under my arm, hands in my pockets. I knew I'd have to get more active soon.

Kelly and I met with Derry in her office for lunch. We had a laughing time, picking things out of brown lunch bags. Kelly went outside to go to the bathroom.

I took the minute to speak to Derry.

"I need to go to your husband," I said.

"No don't," said Derry. Then she added, "You know why."

Yes, I knew why. Because even when dead, somehow love persists.

Chapter 196

I was sitting on the couch in the orphanage lobby. Kelly had borrowed my cane and was limping around like the Mummy, then bursting into a Comanche whoop and whirling the cane overhead. Hilda was at the reception desk, marking ledgers and moving books from one place to another.

Kelly ran up and stopped at my knees.

"What's that? Under your coat? Is it a gun?" he asked.

"It's a squirt gun," I said.

"Do you squirt people with it?" asked Kelly, intrigued.

"No, I kill monsters with it," I said.

"Is it fun?" laughed Kelly.

"Sure is," I said.

Chapter 197

Kelly wanted to play with my squirt gun. I said no. It's much too dangerous to put a neon orange squirt gun into the hands of a child. Much too dangerous for me.

Kelly went back to whooping and running about the lobby with my cane.

He was about twenty feet away, near the lobby door, when suddenly he saw something through the glass door in the parking lot. He dropped the cane and ran out before I could stop him.

I leapt toward the closing door.

There in the concrete drive, a hundred feet away, was Derry's husband, Chuck, kneeling with arms out.

Kelly was running to him.

I threw open the door. Behind Chuck stood three more of Heirpat's hulking vampires. This time they were in suits, ties, and sunglasses. Well-groomed. For blood suckers. Behind them stood Chuck's black Mercedes with the doors open.

Kelly was shouting, "Daddy!" and running full tilt to his father's arms.

I reached under my jacket and pulled out my squirt gun.

"Hey!" I shouted, waving the gun in the air.

Chuck stiffened on seeing me. The three well-groomed vampires focused menace my.

I had to stop Kelly. I'd never reach them before they swept the boy into the black car.

I jumped down the steps and ran. I had to do something quick.

"Kelly, stop! Your mother wants you!" I shouted.

Kelly's legs came to a halt and he turned to look back.

Kelly's father, face black with rage, yelled as if he were commanding a dog, "Kelly! Come here!"

He stepped forward, but hesitated seeing me running his way.

I tagged Kelly's shoulder. I pushed him behind me, telling him to go to his mother.

The three well-groomed vampires were watching me intently.

Chuck's face was icy and stricken. I could see he didn't want anything to do with me.

Just then Hilda came out the Orphanage front door waving my cane over her head.

"Bill, you dropped your cane!" she shouted. She continued waving my death weapon from the top step.

The sight of two supposed slayers was too much for Chuck. He backed up quickly and jumped into the Mercedes.

The three vampire guards looked at each other, then lumbered back into the car themselves. Four doors slammed. Then the tires screeched.

I was glad to see my reputation proceeded me.

When I got to the top step, Kelly was safely behind Hilda.

I said, "Thanks for bringing out my cane. You look good with it. You should carry one yourself."

"What did Kelly's Dad want?" laughed Hilda.

"Oh, the same old thing," I said.

Chapter 198

I told Derry of Ex-husband Chuck's visit that night in the apartment. Derry's eyes went bleary with anger. Me bringing more upset into her home. But I wanted to use it as evidence that I should pursue Chuck.

"We're inviting vampires into the Home," said Derry, grimacing and looking at the ceiling.

"Perhaps you should take a vacation," I said.

"Meaning what? Where would we go?" asked Derry.

"We stay here. We don't go to the Orphanage. We hole up until something breaks," I said.

The phone rang.

Derry and I looked at each other. Finally she got up and the ringing clipped short as she lifted the receiver.

"Hello?"

Derry stood in silence for several seconds. Then she simply held the phone out to me. She wouldn't look at me.

"What?" I said into the black instrument. Then I heard the raspy voice I was expecting.

"*Soyez le vrais vampire*," growled Heirpat. "What are you, a coward, can't kill humans like the rest of us? Are you looking for weak excuses for killing your own kind? Step up and be a real vampire, Cousin. You can be great, as I am. You can share my realm. I have conquered continents, and you know it. What is your insipid interest in protecting this boy? You'll do nothing but get yourself crucified and staked. I tell a troop of my own to come and take you, and they'll take you. Many against the one. This is your last warning. Leave the boy to us or die."

"I can already see you wiggling on the end of my cane," I said. Then I put down the phone.

"It was him," said Derry. She was shaking just visibly. The voice of menace had just entered her home.

"Yes," I said.

"What did he want?"

"He wants me to be a real vampire and help kill the boy," I said.

Chapter 199

The next day was Saturday and Derry and I thought it best to stay in. Kelly watched cartoons and the Saturday spiel of moronic actions on the TV screen. Ah me, once again I realized the age of wit and white wigs was long dead.

Derry and I sat together for lunch. We got along well, and if it hadn't been for the pressure of all the world's vampires surrounding us, it might have been a fine day.

About 2:00 Kelly was bored and bouncing about the apartment unhappy.

He came up to me.

"Can I play with your squirt gun?"

Derry blinked. And I laughed.

"I don't think so, Kelly. Sorry," I said. I had left the holstered squirt-gun under Derry's bed.

"I'll be right back," I said, "Lock the door."

I left the apartment and went to my lair.

I rummaged around in one of my suitcases until I found it. I went and filled it with tap water.

When I reentered Derry's apartment, I was wearing a plastic yellow sunflower as boutonniere.

"I'm back," I called.

Kelly ran up and asked, "Where did you go?"

"Just out. Want to smell my flower?" I said, bending and offering my lapel.

"Sure!" said Kelly. He put his nose up like a beagle.

I squeezed the little plastic bulb and squirted him right in the snout.

He jumped backed surprised, then laughed, wiping at the water.

"Wow!" he said. "It squirted me!"

"You can have it. I'll show you how it works," I said.

"Cool, can I squirt you?" asked Kelly.

By now I had disengaged the squirt-flower and plastic tube from my coat and was handing it like a dead snake to Kelly's eager hands.

"I think first you ought to go squirt your mother," I said.

"Yeah!" said Kelly.

I hooked him up and sent him off into the kitchen alone on his secret mission.

I heard Derry laugh with good-natured surprise.

Chapter 200

The next day was Sunday and Derry didn't have to go to the Home. We spent a pleasant morning in the kitchen, Kelly still running about the apartment squirting objects with his flower. He had to be helped every five minutes to refill the thing.

"He certainly loves the toy," said Derry.

"Yes," I said.

"What are we doing today?" asked Kelly as he came up smiling and hopeful.

Derry looked across the kitchen table, still in a bathrobe and slippers, her hair slightly mussed, a few lines of care under her eyes.

"Perhaps we should stay indoors," said Derry.

Kelly's face dropped in disappointment.

"Why don't we venture a walk in the park this afternoon?" I said.

Derry looked at me.

"We can't live our lives between four walls, now can we?" I said.

"Yeah!" said Kelly. "Can we go to Stow Lake?"

"Sure, why not. Just a Sunday like any other," I said.

Derry looked at me uneasy.

"Are you sure?" she asked.

"Sitting targets, walking targets, what's the difference?" I said. "We have to claim our place in the sun. I think. Don't you?"

"We certainly do," said Derry.

"Yeah!" Kelly piped in.

Chapter 201

That afternoon, about three o'clock, we got ready to go to the park. Kelly was checking under the couches for his tennis shoes.

I was alone with Derry in her well-lit bedroom.

Derry was brushing her hair preparing for our walk. I was sitting in the background watching this household phenomenon from my distant corner. Privy to the privacy of another, I savored watching her as intent as a cat.

"Bill?" said Derry into the mirror.

"Yes?"

"When and if this is over, if we somehow finish with Heirpat, will you stop your killing of vampires? Will you?"

Derry was thinking ahead to something long-term she wanted between us.

"No," I answered from my corner.

Derry continued brushing her hair, but this time with slightly stiffer strokes.

Chapter 202

The pigeons fell to the ground and began a savage pecking.

With a chapeau that held a clownish yellow rose, an old woman in long gray overcoat was throwing down handfuls of Cheerios impassively.

Kelly ran up and jumped with both feet into the feeding puddle, sending up a splash of startled birds.

The old woman, expression unchanged, continued throwing down the cereal.

"Kelly, don't bother the birds, that lady is feeding them," called Derry.

The old woman with the flower hat never looked up or glanced our way.

People were walking around us on the sidewalk. With good weather, a warm afternoon, the fragrance of fresh cut lawn filled the air as mowers were pushed forward over the park grounds. Kids here and there were kicking soccer balls. Old folks with grey hair and grey expressions were parked humpbacked on park benches. Energetic barefooted collegians in shorts were tempting dogs to leap into the air after frisbees.

We still had a half-mile to walk before the stairs up to Stow Lake.

Kelly was running ahead inspecting the sights.

"Bill?" said Derry, "What is life for a vampire?"

"No limits," I said.

"What do you mean, no limits?"

"Once you're outside the confines of human society, its laws, there are no limits. You can do anything. Anything you have courage for and the stomach to see the consequences of. The landscape of human society falls away, the connections are broken."

"How are the connections broken?"

"Life becomes very long, nearly eternal," I said. "And there's not much to live for when you're eternal."

"I don't get it," said Derry, her forehead wrinkled. "You can't have relationships?"

"Oh, brief connections, eternally broken. Once you live on that plane, you're very aware of how quickly things end. All things loom with their ending. You will always live past them. You live with brief intense encounters and memories. And no limits."

I looked at Derry, "And that's different from a life with a future, a life with hope."

Derry nodded, her expression sour.

"How do you decide what to do?"

"The decisions aren't hard. When life stretches, when you will always outlive your actions, the results become unimportant. It isn't that the decisions are hard or easy. They're useless."

"What do vampires live for?"

"Most break down to following thrills."

"Is that what you do, seek thrills?"

"In my way," I said.

"And let me guess," said Derry, "Yours is the thrill of the hunt."

That raised a smile from me that exposed a toothy canine.

"Dear Derry, if ever you need to drive a stake through my heart," I laughed, "It's okay if you need to twist it a little, too."

"You are hopeless!" said Derry exasperated.

We'd climbed the stairs to Stow Lake, and there it was, an expanse of water filled with a tall wooded island. The water, like most duck ponds, was thickly green. Dipping your hand, it was a green that made your fingertips disappear before your thumb touched the water. Whatever you dropped below the lake's surface was lost for good.

Cat tails and reeds stood in leafy fortresses around the banks. A sidewalk surrounded the entire lake like a flat moat, and people could stroll its circumference in less than twenty minutes, passing park benches and people picnicking on blankets along the way.

Kelly ran to the lake's edge and began looking beneath for living creatures.

Derry and I looked across the water. The lake was patrolled by slow-moving electric speedboats and paddle boats with people leaning back as they pedaled. Stow Lake was actually a large circular channel, at some places 200 feet wide, in other's narrowing to 20 feet where people on the sidewalk could talk without raising their voices to people on the great pine-covered hump, the island with a pagoda on its side.

"Can we do the paddle boats?" called Kelly.

"Sure, why not?" I said.

We walked around to the boathouse and concession stand. On the way, we saw the usual sideshow of Stow Lake sights, lonely individuals feeding gulping fish, parents and toddlers squatting to feed ducks, the eternal American joggers headed for greener parts of the park —even one ambitious young man ran by juggling three neon-orange balls. Kelly stood in awe as the busy young man passed.

"Which do you want to ride, the speedboat or the paddle boat?" asked Derry.

"Paddle boat!" said Kelly.

Derry got in line for a ticket as Kelly and I stood at the lake's concrete edge and looked at the boats. The paddle boats were aqua, egg yolk, or ledger-paper green. They were basically humped fiberglass rafts with two molded seats facing forward like sidecars, where the pedaling was done, and a flat bench in back where passengers sat facing backwards. The whole contraption wallowed low in the water with a healthy promise of damp shoes.

Derry came back with the ticket and a worker in overalls handed us three seat cushions that doubled as life preservers.

"Me in front!" cried Kelly, jumping off the side of the concrete into the boat. He quickly scrambled into one of the pedaler's seats.

"You or me?" asked Derry.

"You," I said.

Derry bent and stepped gingerly onto the boat, seating herself in the other pedaling station. I took my place on the little bench facing backwards. Kelly was already excited and pedaling before I was seated. The concession worker tossed in the little bow rope.

"We've got to turn," said Derry.

"Turn the steel ring," I said to Kelly, who quickly found the tiller between the seats and gave it a twist. The squat little boat made a slow swan turn out toward the lake.

"Let's cross the whole ocean!" said Kelly.

"We're on a lake, Dude," I said, laughing. I looked around on my platform feeling like a man in a wheelchair being ferried across water.

"This is work," said Derry, sinking lower in the seat to ease the pedaling.

"Let's just go slow as we can," I said. "The lake's a pretty place, let's see it."

Kelly cut back on his furious pedaling and we began to cruise at about a duck's speed.

The lake was beautiful in the afternoon light. The water surface was foiled with sparkling sun flashes, the reedy brakes were deep and protective, the island edge darkly shaded with low branches and brush that waded deep into the water.

With seagulls calmly paddling before us, floating high on the water like toy boats, we pedaled for ten minutes clockwise round the island. We went under the first arched bridge, large enough for just the slightest echo to form, passing walking families sidewalk-bound and deep in conversation, and then floated slowly out into the larger expanse of the lake.

"How are the legs?" I asked Kelly.

"Good," he said. But I could see a slight sweat on his brow.

"Mine are turning to rubber," laughed Derry.

"I'll take a turn later," I said.

"Long as we don't tip this boat over when we change seats," said Derry.

"Cool! Can we?" asked Kelly.

"Tip the boat over?" laughed Derry askance, "You're crazy!"

I laughed and laid my cane across my lap comfortably.

"This is pretty easy back here," I said.

Kelly and Derry laughed.

We floated and joked our way into the narrowing back channel of the lake. On a far park bench a man sat obscured by a newspaper held up before him. As we came in nearer the banks, Derry was pointing out the dozens of humped disks of sunning turtles piled like hubcaps on the half-submerged branches and rocks. Kelly was ecstatic, waving his arms to make the sleepy piles move. A floating head or two submerged, suddenly sinking like popbottles, but nothing else happened.

Trees lined both sides of the sleepy back channel, throwing shade that made the water dark. A group of men in black shirts and jeans were sitting and kneeling near the bank, talking with theatrically gesturing hands. I saw several more men and two women walking along the island path toward us on the right. Ahead was the double-arched stone bridge that we must pass under. The two arches were just wide enough that it would take a decision, but not much skill, to steer the boat through.

Derry turned to me, frowning.

"Something's wrong."

I could tell this came straight from her ESP. I looked quickly round. There on the park bench behind us, the sitting man had now lowered his newspaper and was smiling at me. He waved.

"Heirpat," I said.

Derry followed my gaze to where the old vampire was getting up from the bench, calmly folding his newspaper beneath his arm.

"What do we do?" asked Derry.

"Keep pedaling toward the bridge," I said, "but toward the far bank, he's behind us, let's keep moving."

Kelly was looking around at us bewildered by our change of tone.

The lake channel was narrowing as we approached within fifty feet of the bridge. The group of talking men was still kneeling there. We steered slowly toward the bank opposite them.

"Bonjour! Comment ca va!" called Heirpat, "Are you having a happy day?" The old vampire was now picking up his pace hurrying along the sidewalk. I looked up at the island bank some ten feet away. The walking group on the island was now turning down toward us. I could see their faces.

"Steer away from the bank," I said. I reached forward and steered us back into the middle of the channel.

Derry looked at me questioningly.

"Vampires," I said, head tilted toward the group now treading down the leafy branches and leaves to the water's edge.

The men kneeling near the bridge were standing up and spreading out along the other bank. Heirpat had passed us and was on the bridge directly ahead of us.

"Stop paddling," I said.

"Yes, a fine day!" called Heirpat from the mid-bridge, leaning over the thick stone rail watching us. He was happy with the spectacle.

Sitting ducks, what an apt phrase.

"Bill!" cried Derry, pointing to the other bank.

I gripped my cane and looked around. The group of vampires in black were already wading knee-deep, trudging toward us. The other group on our right was now waist deep, plodding with arms up, eyes intent and savagely focused our way.

"What's happening? Why are they in the water? Do they want our boat?" asked Kelly.

"Back pedal, fast," I urged. I crouched on the little boat's stern, but realized it was a hopelessly tippy platform for spearing vampires.

I heard Heirpat laugh caustically.

"Ah, my, are you having trouble there? Perhaps my friends can help you off your little boat!"

"Give me you squirt gun!" commanded Derry.

"That's the spirit," I said. I took out my squirt gun, doffed the duct tap from the nozzle, and handed it over just as the enclosing group of vampires were getting within arm's reach of her.

"One squirt each," I said. "I'll take care of the ones on this side." I gripped the rubber handgrip of my cane tightly and leaned toward the oncoming threats.

The vampires on both sides were now just savage faces and hands raised and moving toward us, their chests beneath the green water. With their chests out of sight it was going to be iffy business trying to stake even one before they tipped us. The first one lunged to the side of the boat as Derry raised my trusty weapon and pumped the trigger.

The orange squirt gun gave a dry fizz.

"It's empty!" shouted Derry. "It's empty!"

I looked from the empty gun to Kelly grimacing and shrinking guiltily in his seat.

"Of course, with so many," called Heirpat, "You won't even know which one is holding him under!"

"Bill! Bill!" said Derry scooting back as if snake bitten.

I reached into my inner pocket and took out the small vile I always kept on me. It was identical to the one I had given Derry for killing vampires. I uncorked it with my bare hands and ever so carefully tossed it into the water.

"Backup, don't let them splash us," I shouted. "Pedal! Pedal!"

Wide-eyed, Derry began pedaling even as the first vampire hand reach into the boat for her leg. That set her pedaling with a superhuman kicking.

And then the toxin took effect. The water turned to a frothy boil of screaming, plunging vampires, twisting like dying crocodiles, gargling in their own vomiting juices, torsos filled with spasmodic contortions as a few child's tears in the green lake scalded them to death.

A few were jumping up and down in the water like crazed Jack-In-The-Boxes.

It was quite a sight. And I would have enjoyed it if I hadn't been sitting petrified, perched with my feet up on the seat of the little boat. One splash and I knew I'd be right in there raving with them. Cooking in a cauldron of vampire soup.

"*Merde, petit cons, qu'est ca tu a fait!*" Hierpat was screaming from the top of the bridge.

The last hands of the dead vampires were now sinking with twitching fingers like people calling for cabs.

"Please," I said to Derry, "Pedal out of here slowly. I can't let any of this lake water touch me or..."

"Okay, okay, no problem," said Derry, taking the steering ring in her hand and backing away from the bridge the way we had come.

For nearly a minute I heard Heirpat cawing his hate at us. Then we slipped around the island out of sight, passing where the little pagoda stood in utter quiet and seemingly eternal calm.

Kelly was in tears.

"Those were bad people," he said sniffing. Derry was pedaling, stern with concentration.

"No kidding," said Derry.

"Bill, are you okay?" she asked.

270

"I hope you won't mind if I don't take my turn pedaling back," I said. I was squatting on two feet like a leather-coated owl on a branch. I held my cane with its laughing doggy face stabbed down in front of me for balance. I cast my eye around me for any stray water-droplets that might have landed on the boat during the dying commotion. I didn't see any and I hoped for no little surprises.

"Where did those people go?" asked Kelly, mystified.

"I really don't care," I said.

Chapter 203

I made a magnificent leap from the little boat high onto the pavement, safe, and none of the ever-tolerant San Franciscans even made a remark, over-used to such theatrics. Derry got Kelly out of the boat and we hurried him away as fast as his little legs would carry him.

I didn't think Heirpat would attack, because he wouldn't be coming after me alone.

Still, both Derry and I were relieved when we finally closed and locked her apartment door. Derry plopped down on the couch exhausted.

I went and sat down beside her a bit morose.

Kelly turned around in the apartment unsure what to do.

Then he walked up to Derry and I and stood.

"Mom, can we do it again?" he asked.

Derry and I looked at each other as he stood scowling, worried that he was now eternally cut off from riding the boats in the park.

Then like a killer comedian he said, "Why are you laughing?"

Chapter 204

Derry understandably was shaky and nervous the rest of the day. I helped Kelly keep occupied. At one point we all sat slumped shouldered in front of the TV. But neither Derry or I were watching the program. We had inner landscapes we were tending

Finally, as Derry and I cleared the dinner plates from the table, she turned to me plate in hand like an usher taking a church offering.

"Can't we just run away? Can't we?" pleaded Derry. "He's going to come after you, too."

"No," I said. "I'm must do something about him."

"Because you're into it. You want to do this."

"Don't worry, I'm going to kill Heirpat," I said.

Derry asked, "Why you?"

"His evil must be stopped," I replied.

"What's the difference? What's the difference if he's running around killing people and you're running around killing people, too?"

"At least I have the honor of killing other vampires," I said.

"Ah," said Derry in mock wonder, "The honor of the military."

I didn't like it, but it was true.

Chapter 205

I'd tried knocking on his door and he hadn't been very cordial, so I decided this time to go in the back way. Give Derry's husband a little surprise.

Out of pity, I thought I might just do this with my cane.

I jumped the back fence from the alley. It was head high, tall enough that once I was over I was sure none of the neighbors could see me. I didn't want to be mistaken as a prowler and have the cops busting in while I was half finished with my work.

The backyard was standard lawn, bushes, and a swing set. On the back porch twelve steps went up steeply to a back door with a tiny window pane.

When I tried it, the door wasn't locked.

I stepped in, looking around, finding I was in a laundry room. Seems like I was doing a lot of business near laundries lately. The next door showed me the kitchen.

There at a kitchen table sat Derry's husband, smoking a cigar, and reading a brochure.

"Thinking of making an investment in Hawaii?" I asked.

Derry's husband jumped sideways out of his chair as if I'd dumped boiling water on him. The chair somersaulted and skidded across the floor.

He grabbed up a long butcher knife from the counter and threw it at me. It missed, but stuck in the wall beside me.

"Pure luck," I said, admiring the knife wagging like a dog tail next to me.

"Get away!" shouted Derry's husband. He ran.

"Dont' forget your little investment paper about paradise!" I shouted.

Sure, gruesome, but I was having fun.

I strode into the living room. Derry's husband was busy working at the inside locks and latches of the front door. They were delaying his escape and he was having trouble with them. He was squinting and grimacing as he tugged at the door.

I grabbed him by the collar and threw him over the couch. He sat up, doing a crabwalk to the far wall.

I walked over and stood before him.

"Let's talk," I said.

He only swallowed at that.

"Stand up," I said.

Again he only swallowed, as if he were choking on his own fate.

I reached down, grabbed his shirt, and stood him up against the living room wall.

"Derry says hello," I said. "You'd forgotten her, didn't you?"

274

He blinked and looked at me as best he could.

"What do you want?" he croaked.

I love croakers.

"Where is Heirpat?"

"I don't know who you're talking about."

I whipped my cane across his face, bringing up a red welt thick as a garden hose. He grabbed his cheek as if to catch the pain.

I pushed him up against the wall, stepped back, then rammed my cane all the way through the wall, just beside his armpit.

His mouth dropped open as he looked down at my weapon, speared next to his chest. He stood there something like the man the magician throws knives at in a carnival.

"I don't know where he's at," said Derry's husband. This time it was the truth.

I jerked my cane from the wall. It came out with a little pop and puff of white drywall like an infinitely small gunshot.

"Where's your little friend who brought you across?"

He pursed his lips in some kind of macho protection. He shook his head.

Mistake.

"Macho is just clinging to the evil old method of male subjugation," I said.

"Okay, okay, she's coming back tomorrow," he pleaded.

"Tomorrow is a long ways away for you. I don't think you'll ever get there," I smiled.

Then I staked him. Hard.

Chapter 206

I suppose theoretically I should feel pity for Chuck, the Real Estate Agent, who divided up the earth into little squares to buy from the misery of some and sell to the rich luck of others, who fell for the temptation of his receptionist as he bustled the paperwork of land rights from one place to another, who forgot his family and loved ones, and lost them in the process. But I don't. In that way, I am like Buddha, I accept the role of suffering in the world. Perhaps a step beyond Buddha. Accepting that our sufferings are luminescent teachers, that it makes no difference what you are reborn as in the next life (I simply granted him that chance to get on with his next rebirth) that if you are reborn a dog, you have a dog's problems, that if you are reborn a pig, you have pig problems, that if you fall for a vampire, you suffer vampire problems. And I'm simply the larger instrument of the world's suffering, benevolent or malicious, it makes no difference.

Yeah, that sounds good.

Chapter 207

Oh, Derry, and you are so beautiful, loving, and forgiving.

And I am so not so.

Chapter 208

Love. What was it to me? I recalled a mangled vampire poem I had once written:

The Mail

I wrapped up a big ball of disease and Christian love
in butcher paper and mailed it, care of Father Sierra, to
California Native Americans.
No reply.

I shoveled AIDS, Syphilis, Gonorrhea in a heavy box
and mailed it to those stumbling and struggling
with unaccepted loves.
No response.

I salted a holocaust into
an envelope and mailed it to the thirsty Jews.
No answer.

I stuffed sparking atomic materials into a steel cylinder
and dropped it off at Nagasaki.

No word after the thunder.

So I wrote my love on a flimsy post card and
mailed it to those closest to my breast.
It came back : Return to Sender
Addressee Unknown
No Forwarding Address.

For me there was no forwarding address, in more ways than one.

Chapter 209

When I entered Derry's apartment it was strangely quiet. Kelly was sitting crossed-legged next to the TV, turned down to barely audible, watching and fiddling with his squirt flower. I checked the kitchen, but she wasn't there, then I noticed Derry's bedroom door was closed.

Time to deliver bad news. I knocked ever so lightly.

I heard a muffled reply, so I gently opened the door and slipped in. I closed the door tight behind me.

Derry was sitting upright on the edge of her bed, looking out at the blue patch of her window.

I hesitated before speaking, but Derry turned, and I saw there were tears already in her eyes.

"I went to your old house in the Sunset," I started.

Derry merely shook her head.

She was way ahead of me. Her face was full of pain.

I nodded and left the room.

Chapter 210

I stepped out of the room and returned to Kelly sitting before the TV. I sat on the couch behind him.

The TV was blithering on.

It wasn't much of a babysitter.

"You know, the TV isn't a good teacher," I said to Kelly. He turned at the waist to look at me.

"Why?"

"Oh, because you don't learn what normal life is like. You see implausible cartoons, you see extremes of behavior, people getting too angry, too drunk, you see wars and the disasters of politics. The news is bad. The world tottering on calamity. Some triumphs, some victory, much pain. The false adventure of guns. But what's normal life, where is it on the TV?"

Kelly nodded, didn't understand, and went back to watching the TV.

Stupid lectures from the vampirical world. I'd seen my own exploits on TV once or twice myself.

I just needed to talk.

Chapter 211

In the early morning blackness, I got up leaving Derry's warm bed. She budged and looked up sleepily, her hair falling in tangles. She'd been so exhausted that night she'd slept without knowing I'd come in and was beside her.

"You're getting up?" she said, blinking.

I told Derry I was going out again. She must keep the door locked and not answer it.

"Where are you going?" she asked.

"Back to your old house," I said.

"Did you learn anything from my...from Chuck?" asked Derry.

"His receptionist will come to the house today. I expect to learn something more from her," I said. "She will be the one who brought Chuck across."

Derry nodded.

"Bill?"

"Yes?"

"Did Chuck suffer?" Derry asked. I could see Derry had been impressed by the vampires raving and dying in the lake.

"Only as a vampire," I said, "Before that he had you."

Chapter 212

Just before I left, on a whim, I asked Derry to check her ESP and tell me if I needed to duck any oncoming harpoons.

"No, only something strange," said Derry, running her fingers back from her forehead through her tangled hair.

"Better tell me," I said.

"You may see your daughter," said Derry.

I grunted and swallowed, grimacing at the unbelieveable. My poor daughter was years dead. I had buried her by scraping out dirt with my bare hands.

I turned to go.

"Bill, be careful. Come back? Please?"

I turned but didn't say it would be someone else who wouldn't be coming back.

Derry put her face up. She wanted me to kiss her.

But I couldn't and I left with Derry pulling the covers tighter around her.

Chapter 213

I sat in the darkened window of Derry's house. I'd disposed of Chuck in a dumpster, as is my norm. Now I merely sat looking out on the neighborhood, watching from a darkened recess as morning rose.

Derry's old house was large and comfortable. Spacious rooms with walls taken back to the least necessary. Overstuffed furniture. A wooden staircase running steeply up to the bedrooms upstairs. The banister was painted white, the stairs carpeted. I'd had time to look around as I waited for Chuck's little friend.

My perch was the bench of a large bay window, giving me a good view of the street below, my cane lying casually across my lap. I thought about Derry as I waited for an unknown woman to appear.

I thought about love. A sorry topic for a vampire.

I thought how it passes from one human to another, from man to woman, woman to man, woman to woman, man to man, without consideration for the bounds of propriety or color of a face. It sprang from admiration, joy of fellowship, the possibility of caring. It was ephemeral, moved without knowing, sightless, untamed. Cherished. And so destructive when lost. I had to admire the destructive part.

You people left without love can appreciate that.

Chapter 214

Instead of her normal white, she was in a black jumpsuit that looked like leather but was actually an artificial hide. Her black hair was long and free, dividing into serpents rolling over her shoulders, and her shapely walk accented enough to make the large zipper ring at her neck wag. The zipper in the hide suit ran from her neck to her crotch. I recognized her even as she walked out of the park and began wagging this way. Now that she was at the turn into Derry's sidewalk, I didn't like what I saw.

I could feel my anger rising. Bad sign.

There was a quiet knock on the door. At least this time I had the choice of opening it.

I swung the door open and stood full face before her.

Her reaction was something like mine. Startled to recognize me.

"*Guillaume, c'est toi?*" she gulped. Her white hands had come back to her chest in bunny paws as she stepped back.

"Tala," I said. I grabbed the vampiress who'd brought me across by the chest of her jump suit and dragged her in.

Chapter 215

She squealed and began clawing at me. She was wriggling, hissing, and raking her nails at me face. Fortunately I had her at arms length. In my other hand I held my cane down and ready.

"Let me go you little sucking pig!" spat Tala.

"*C'est bon de vous revoir tambien*" I said. "Hold still!"

I breathed in slowly to put down my emotion. If Tala caught wind of it, she would come at me.

Tala ceased her struggling. Her eyes sharpened and I could see her begin thinking.

"You are so much stronger than the little vampire I left so long ago," she smiled. "But I do remember you, Guillaume. I remember much about you, every part of your body."

"I remember as well," I said. "No one every really recovers from it, I'm sure."

I pushed Tala down hard into an easy chair that squatted behind her. Her head banged back against the shoulder as she landed. But she recovered quickly. She squelched back a curse as she watched me.

Two predators wondering who would eat whom.

"What brings you here?" asked Tala. Her voice was the same throaty robust call.

"The same old story. Your husband, Heirpat, of course."

"Ah, but you never met him, did you?" she smiled.

"I have recently. It's always nice to meet the person who's going to kill you prior to your death."

"He's going to kill you? Why?" asked Tala, smiling her snaky smile. Her black eyes were looking deeply into mine. Searching.

"No, I'm going to kill him," I said.

"My you have become the ambitious little vampire," laughed Tala. "But you'd better mind your own business, or he'll hand you your empty heart on a stick."

"So he's told me," I said.

"So what have you been doing with yourself all these years?" she said, "I haven't seen you."

"You wouldn't be here if I had," I said.

"Ah, my, you're a..." Tala hesitated. She raised her chin and smiled.

"A slayer," I said.

"Stinking breed," she said regally. "Giving up the pleasure we've afforded you for fatal pursuits."

"You and Heirpat would know intimately about fatal pursuits," I said.

"Now I understand. You're the one Heirpat mentioned is keeping him from the boy."

I smiled guardedly.

"Ah," laughed Tala, shaking back her hair and pushing out her bosom, "Now I understand. Heirpat can't understand why you would protect this boy. But that's not your real reason, it is? You're not protecting the boy. You're after something else."

"I don't need a real reason," I said. "Like you, I just act upon what I want. Which is to know where Heirpat is," I said.

"Oh?" said Tala, her beautiful black eyebrow raised in mock-surprise.

I carefully extended my cane and placed the tip at the sternum of her jumpsuit.

Tala stifled a wince of fear. She blinked a moment realizing her grave danger. Then she looked at me and smiled.

Her hand raised to her neck and she pulled the little ring. She unzipped her suit letting her beasts escape, pulling it down until I could see the black tangles of her pubic mound.

Her belling undulated once like a snake.

She looked upon me, smiling, in her vampire calling.

The vampire who brings you across always has powers over you.

"No," I said gruffly. I took the cane in my two hands and pressed the tip until it threatened to penetrate Tala's skin.

She grimaced, eyes squinting. She was struggling to hold her seductrice's gaze.

"Where is Heirpat or die," I said.

Tala swallowed. She knew she was in trouble. She also must have known that if she told me she was dead.

Her penetrating eyes left me. She bowed her head. And when her face came back up, it was a face I knew.

There, upon Tala's exposed body, was may wife's face, looking at me, pleading. Tala had taken on her features to feed me a douse of my own pain. "Guillaume, don't. We can be happy again together," said Tala through my wife's lips.

"Where is Heirpat?" I screamed, my rage flooding me. I was nearly out of control.

I could feel Tala strengthen before me. An ancient vampiress gaining girth. Feeding once again from me.

Leaving the tip of my cane on her chest, I put out my shaking hand and took her by the throat.

Tala's eyes closed with pain. Her mouth opened from suffocation. And then I saw her features changing again. Changing from the warm and welcome of my dead wife, to a look of childish pain, of innocent bewilderment and anguish.

And there I saw the face of my own daughter.

"Don't, don't kill me, please Father!" said my daughter.

I closed my eyes and put the stake entirely through the spectre, the chair, and my loss.

Chapter 216

Tala's arms rose waving over her head, her mouth open and soundless. It was something like the sight of a three-headed snake writhing in death agony.

Finally she quit flopping.

I looked at her, stake between her beautiful breasts and her exposed navel.

I had still wanted her.

Oh, if only I could have been a cat and just vomit up my own insides.

I thought for a moment of drinking my little vial of children's tears and having done with it right there.

Chapter 217

I sat for a long time in the bay window, merely breathing in and out. Nearly an hour it took to attain my normal chill. Without it, I would be a dead vampire shortly. I had nearly let Tala feed off my little secret garden of rage. That door must be locked and hidden. Hidden from other prying vampire eyes.

Finally I went back to her and drew my cane from her chest.

She fell forward like a flour sack onto the floor.

I noticed a small zippered pocket on her hip.

I unzipped it.

Within was only a slip of paper. It read:

Jimmy Johnson, 555-3737

Chapter 218

When I stepped into Derry's hallway, I thought, "Strange door mat."

Then I looked and saw it was a body collapsed at Derry's doorstep.

I rushed to Derry's door.

There lay a small dead vampire. A dwarf complete in kid's suit and tie, lying on his back, dead, eyes and mouth open as if to catch a rain that would never fall in the hallway. Oddly a Bible lay sedately by his side.

"Derry!" I shouted and pushed on the door. It was still locked. I took out Derry's key and entered the apartment.

As I looked around the living room was still in order, no overturned chairs, no sign of disturbance.

"Derry!" I called. "It's Bill!"

Derry's bedroom door opened and first Kelly then Derry rushed out to me.

"Oh, you're back. Thank god!" said Derry.

"Mom had to kill somebody!" whispered Kelly. He was uncertain whether this was good or bad news.

"What happened? I said.

"While you were out, there was a knock on the door. I looked out and there were two men. They wanted me to open the door. Jehovah's witnesses."

"Yeah, real bad Jehovah's witnesses," said Kelly, obviously excited now to be telling a great story.

"I wouldn't open the door," said Derry. "Then they started really pounding. I knew they'd break in and get us. We couldn't get out! So I got your little vial and I opened it. I quietly unlocked the door, jerked it open, and threw the vial out. There was a little one I didn't see under the peephole. It hit him in the face. I just slammed the door and locked it."

"Then lots of yelling!" said Kelly.

"I was so frightened," said Derry.

"And lots of kicking!" cried Kelly practically with glee.

"Well, you got him," I said.

"I thought the others would just come busting in. So I yelled I had a lot more where that came from, I yelled it through the closed door. And they went away."

"You did good," I said.

"Yeah, real good," nodded Kelly.

"Now what? I'm at my wit's end," said Derry.

"We have to leave," I said.

"Where will we go?" asked Derry.

"I know a place. And it's unlikely Heirpat will think to look there for us."

"When will we go?" Derry asked.

"Where are we going?" asked Kelly.

"We'll go as soon as I change your doormat," I said. "Pack your clothes."

Kelly was instantly running to his room as if I'd promised a vacation.

I put my arm around Derry's shoulder and squeezed. Trying to put some life back into her.

She shook her head and left for her room.

I got a blanket then went out to dumpster a dwarf.

(That old time religion wasn't good enough for him.)

Chapter 219

I brought the yellow Volvo station wagon around, then went up and carted down Derry's two hastily packed suitcases. At the same time I had retrieved my squirt guns. Finally I went back up and walked Kelly and Derry down to the car. Kelly was carrying a small brown bag.

"What's in the bag?" I asked.

"My squirt flower," said Kelly. He opened it to show me.

"I'm glad you brought that, you're going to need it," I smiled.

We got in the car. Derry sat mum in her seat, staring forward, as I prepared to drive away from her flower-covered home. Kelly eagerly buckled his seat belt as if preparing for a carnival ride.

I drove off at a leisurely pace.

At first, I drove all over the city so no one could follow us.

Then I swung back around via Taraval toward the Sunset.

"That's our old house!" shouted Kelly as I pulled up in the drive, going back as far out of sight of the street as I could.

Derry looked out, wide-eyed at the old stucco fortress.

"But Chuck and his girlfriend live there!" cried Derry.

"Not any more," I said.

Chapter 220

It took some convincing to get Derry to go in.

"It's your old home, you need to live there, no matter what went on in the past," I said. "There are no vampires here, and Heirpat won't expect us to be here."

"Let's go in, Mom," said Kelly impatiently.

"I'm not going to see anything I don't want to see in there?"

Derry's trepidation was earnest.

"You can't exactly consider me as a maid service, but it's honest work," I said.

Derry snorted. Finally she shrugged and we went in.

Chapter 221

I walked Derry from room to room to show her there were no spooks.

She noted small changes in furniture, but not much else. She did stop by the fireplace, spotting the two fresh holes in the drywall.

"I wonder what made that?" she mused.

I didn't tell her it was where I played mubley-peg with her husband.

Kelly moved right into his old room. He went about playing with the toys that were still there, sitting on one of the two beds, one of which was conspicuously empty.

Derry came in, first checking that the window on the back alley was locked. Then sitting down beside Kelly to give him a hug.

Finally, Derry had me walk her up a flight of dark stairs that ascended from the second story to a door that opened onto the roof. When we went out, we were greeted by a clothes line, a few clothespins perched at exhausted angles like emaciated birds, and a great view of the Sunset district and Golden Gate park that stretched almost to the sea. Derry walked once around the tarry surface, assuring herself no vampires were lurking in the gutters, then smiled and nodded at me, and we descended inside again.

After several hours we were settled in. I'd moved the car out of the driveway. On doing so, I went to a local grocery store and bought a week's provisions. I parked the car several blocks away, and made several trips, hopping the back fence to bring the food up the back steps and into the kitchen.

I didn't want unwanted eyes accidentally spotting us coming and going in the house, if possible.

Kelly, Derry, and I put the groceries away, Derry telling us where everything went in cupboards and drawers, just like a real family.

Chapter 222

That night, after Kelly had gone to bed, I confessed to Derry that Chuck's mistress had turned out to be the vampire Tala. And that I'd killed her.

"Your old nemesis," said Derry stiffly.

"Yes," I said.

"And you killed her here?"

"Oh, yes," I said. I was uncomfortable with this ugly scenario.

"So, in a sense you avenged yourself," said Derry.

"Yes," I said. "But that's not the worst part."

"Things could be worse?" asked Derry.

I confessed to Derry that even as I'd skewered Tala, I'd wanted her.

"The roots of your black history run deep," said Derry after some time. "I'm sorry, Bill. But you made your decision, you killed her."

"As usual," I said.

"So now that you have avenged yourself, do you want to leave us? You can. Now that one of your reasons for this quest is done," Derry looked at me neutrally, allowing me to leave if I chose.

"You're wrong twice," I said. "There's still Heirpat, and I must protect the boy from him."

"Did you find anything out from this Tala?" asked Derry.

"Only this," I said. I took out the slip of paper that said Jimmy Johnson and a phone number.

"Who is this?" asked Derry.

"I don't know," I said.

"Well, only one way to find out."

Derry stood up and went over to the phone. She picked up the receiver and tapped the number.

"Hello?" she said. Then she stood listening.

"Could I speak to Jimmy Johnson?"

Derry stood a long while.

"Thank you," and she replaced the phone.

She came back and sat down.

"It was the number to the San Francisco City Jail. I couldn't speak to Jimmy Johnson, because prisoner calling hours are over."

"I'll have to visit in person," I said.

Chapter 223

Derry and I washed the dishes together. We stood comfortably side by side like two horses in a stall.

Chapter 224

I remember a dream I'd once had years back. I was lost at sea in a little rowboat. Heirpat was standing on the bow, holding up his arms, grasping a black cape that he was using as a sail. I sat below him with my back turned slaving at the oars.

I woke up trembling, feeling the need to be part of something.

Chapter 225

Derry and I were having tea in her kitchen. We were sitting, hands around our cups like card players in a stiff silent match. Derry's forehead was slightly wrinkled, hitched with concerns, as she considered our situation. I supposed considering the potential outcomes of being involved with me.

"Bill?' she finally asked.

"Yes, Derry?"

"Why do you kill other vampires? Why do you follow this horrid pursuit?"

"It's a pursuit that protects you," I said.

"No, it's not about me. Why do you do it?"

I thought a moment.

Slightly irritated, I said, "It's the only way I have left to express love for loved ones."

I should have said my *once* loved ones.

Derry pulled back in her chair. She didn't believe it.

"Your loved ones are dead. You show them nothing by it."

"Perhaps," I said.

"Are you expressing some sort of love for me with this slaughter?" asked Derry.

"No," I said.

Derry nodded slightly as if confirming something to herself. But she was not going to let me off.

"Why then? What's in it for you?"

I swallowed, a monster cornered in the small room of my own black being.

"Because expressing my hate is better than expressing nothing."

"Your blind!"

I remained silent.

"You live in such poverty!" cried Derry exasperated.

"I'm sorry, Derry," I said. Of course, it was true.

I could stand it no longer. I got up and left the room.

Then I heard her call behind me.

"And it's all because you believe you are alone."

Chapter 226

Derry's words had sunk deep. I had to look hard at myself, something never easy for a vampire.

Was that my job, transformed by evil, to eternally kill to combat evil? I was part of the vision of evil, an eternal stalker of vampires in the blackness. A bringer of agony, a vampire juicer with three speeds.

And I realized we should take pity on all criminals and police, enemies and armies alike, who take part in the process of evil, for their rewards are doomed to blackness and heartache.

For me, I could predict no happy results. None whatsoever. Ugliness, blackness, they were to be eternally on my hands because I had succumbed to the vision of evil, become part of its process, forever the doer-in of the damned.

I don't want to be! I don't want this sentence to earthly hell. I am not my vampire's-keeper!

Unfortunately, I am my vampire's killer.

And it's nearly impossible for a vampire to stop.

From my point of view, I know of only one way. And there, against the wall, is the doggy head of my cane laughing at me!

Chapter 227

In the four-thirty morning blackness, I got up and left her bedroom. I stole up the black stairs to Derry's roof. I walked silently, the silence of a vampire, around the roof looking out from the three-story view. Only the white bug eyes of a few vehicles were plying the city streets. Across the way, the vast expanse of the Golden Gate park sat dark and waiting. Roaming grounds in the early morning for the walking dead like me. The great spiked structure of Sutro Tower, like a Japanese warrior headress, blinked on the distant hillside behind me with its aerial lights red and angry.

And West was the great blank ocean shrouded with fog moving my way.

I stood at the edge of the roof, this roof from which I could jump but never die. This endless need would be carried on by me and my vampire kin forever. I stood and I looked out across the city waiting for the sun to rise.

Why was I this carrier of anger?

Why was I this righter of wrongs?

And as the pale purple of the East turned to pink and crimson and finally the arched brilliant seam of orange then gold sun, I thought of why I was what I was.

Because I was angry at love denied me.

Chapter 228

And I realized if I was merciless, it was because I had no mercy on myself. If I was without compassion, it was because I had no compassion for myself. I suspected to ever heal I would need to pay closer heed to my inner miseries. I would need to again look in the mirror and see the poor monster on the other side.

But I'm a hardened vampire. A monster. Ha, what a ridiculous image: a vampire feeling sorry for himself.

No. I have only my eternal hate. For me, for my vampire brethren. I'm convicted in my hatred for Heirpat.

And I would pursue him until death!

Chapter 229

The jail guard patted me down, but surprisingly didn't take my cane. He only inspected it, twisting the doggy handle foolishly, to see if a blade was hidden within. Then he smiled at me, and handed it back, content that it was an innocent stick.

I accepted my happy instrument of war with a grateful nod.

I wondered who I'd be seeing as I entered the visitors foyer and had the door locked behind me. A sign overhead the door said ring for attendant.

The other side of the room was a squad of squat phone booths. The booths were small desks with side panels for privacy and a phone. A chair at each desktop looked through a thick plexiglass window into another room where another squat booth sat in a mirror image.

The guard said number 1, then he settled himself against the wall to wait. It looked like his favorite wall for waiting.

I sat down at the first booth and waited.

After several minutes, the door on the opposite side of the glass opened soundlessly. A guard motioned an old man in jail clothing in. I took my first look at Jimmy Johnson.

Casting his eye quickly down the booths, he too saw me. He put back his head and laughed from his grizzled chin.

"Well done!" I heard him shout through the thick glass. It was a faint shout through the deadening pane.

The guard was looking from me to Heirpat with great suspicion.

Heirpat sat down at my booth and casually lifted the phone.

"You found me," he said with glee as I put the receiver to my ear.

"The joy is all yours," I said.

"I was expecting my mistress, Tala," smiled Heirpat. "Although it's nice to see you as well."

"She won't be coming," I said.

That set Heirpat blinking and thinking.

"Yes," I said, leaning toward the glass. I gave it a cheery little finger tap at Heirpat's chest level.

Chapter 230

"So I killed yours and now you've killed mine," said Heirpat.

"*Toute va bien,*" I said.

"Let's not be childish about this," cautioned Heirpat with much cynicism in his yellow eyes, "The occasion of a mate's loss is of great import."

"And fun to behold," I spat back.

"And you've been such a busy bee," laughed Heirpat.

"A vampire's work is never done," I said.

"Well, it is fun exchanging epithets, but do you have anything original to say to me? Something I haven't heard in the past century *ad nauseum*, young lout?"

"Look at you, a prisoner in your own realm," I said.

Heirpat laughed loudly. A laugh supercilious and dismissive.

Chapter 231

"A prisoner? No! The rich and powerful, they come and go as they please, even in here. I simply call a lawyer who takes me out on furlough. I come and go as I want. This is one of my lairs that I feel most relaxed and protected in. I am surrounded by my own. No one can touch me. I have other lairs, of course, I'm a general in a military base whose location I shan't disclose, I am a secret captain of industry in Japan, even dabbling in the Yakuza, a communist leader, African colon, ah, I spread my broad influence to everywhere, even from here. Here, where I'm protected, surrounded by my own. Untouchable!"

"I'd like to touch you," I said.

"Ha," laughed Heirpat, "I'm home. None can reach me here, you can't affect me. *Meme pas l'execution puex me toucher!* Besides, they never execute the immensely rich and powerful. And they wouldn't know how to execute me if they did!"

"I could help them out," I said.

"No, they can't legally let you in," said Heirpat with smirking head tilt.

We sat as two vampires staring from each side of the glass.

"There's nothing you can do to me on your side of the glass. And on my side of the glass, there's no reason for me to change or worry," said Heirpat.

"Except the boy," I said.

Hierpat gave me a smile that rose like a scorpion's tail.

Chapter 232

"He's on your side of the glass and I'll take care of him. On this side, I have wealth, power, an endless supply of victims coming in, ripe for my armies. And centuries of time behind and before me."

"You sound like a happy little addict with an endless supply," I said.

"And you, what's so different for you on your side of the glass?" asked Heirpat savagely. "Oh! I forgot! Tala told me you were of the womanly persuasion. You're probably fucking the boy's mother, aren't you! *Suceur des ses grand nenes*!"

I stood up and the chair fell over behind.

I rammed my cane with all my might into the plexiglass at Heirpat's chest.

With a great crack, the silver cane tip smashed a conical shard from the glass and then a deep peeling scratch, but didn't penetrate.

I felt the guard fall on my back.

Heirpat was standing now, backing away from the damaged glass and laughing.

I threw off the guard as Heirpat cawed at me.

"*A bientot!*" I heard him shout. "*L'anilation! Pour tois, la femme, et le gosse! Je te envois mon amour!*""

When I turned and faced the guard, he didn't like what he saw. He got up, ran to the door, rang until it was unlocked, then ran out.

I walked out behind him.

Well, Hierpat was right in this, even the police couldn't stop me.

Chapter 233

I returned to Derry's house. My rage had subsided.

Hopping the back fence, I went up the stairs and entered the kitchen. I looked around and Derry and Kelly weren't there.

On the kitchen table I found a note from Derry saying they were going to check on Johnny. Derry promised to be careful. They would return by 12:00 o'clock. It was five minutes to high noon and so I decided to wait.

I went to the front window and sat looking out.

I knew that I didn't have to pursue Heirpat anymore. He would come to us.

Chapter 234

I was one more vampire looking out on the world through glass.

Whether I had minutes or centuries to kill, it didn't matter.

Chapter 235

I used to ponder why there was evil in the world. And I had come up with a kind of explanation, a view. If you believed in karma, the results of all our actions carrying on and coming back to us, then I could see on an evolutionary scale why evil exists. Why humans are in the endless struggle to be divorced from it in their becoming. Evil sprang from the long terrible effect of the animal world upon us. The glaring hard golden eye of the lion that sprang, tearing away swatches of flesh from our backs. The hyena dragging away a crying child. The snake's darting stab. The animal world of famine, pain, starvation, and disease, of grasping territoriality to ensure a food supply: that animal existence was part of our history. The animal world which reeked death on others to survive. Which froze and howled at night. Which licked its wounds alone waiting to die. Which formed into killing packs, which formed us into packs.

How could humans not be a reflection of this long suffering, this evolutionary obstacle course and survival run, where hardship and pain were endured with more and more striving? Striving against the blackness of this age-old animal cruelty, which we were part of and came from, which we carried inside us. Our ancient pain, this summary of the karma of an unruly world, hardened our hearts, shaped a reactive consciousness that we wielded as weapons against encroaching animals, and against ourselves! Evil was part of our history because we had slept with wolves! We'd eaten loathsome bugs to survive. We'd killed the children of the next tribe! We slaughtered not one or a hundred buffalo, but millions, leaving our fellows, the Indians to die and dry like cornstalks in a field. Our endless karmic sins were vast. This is where evil came from. This history of our pain. No baby was born with it. No individual was the root. The source of our blackness was deep and ancient and thriving and thirsty. You were not safe. It could come up behind you in the dark and brush your neck like a feather. A black feather that brings home the shiver of harm.

But was it inescapable? We could certainly raise no armies like a wall to keep it out. It was already within. It was already among us.

And we vampires, we were its best soldiers.

Hellion dogs bringing forth the past.

But I remembered seeing in the mirror Derry's beautiful naked body. Her welcoming smile. The hugs given ceaselessly and freely to the surrounding arms of her orphan children. Her full-throated laugh. This woman somehow stood naked before the mirror without this needless shawl of the past.

And she had infused in her children something that made them special indeed:

A love that welled up in their blood.

Chapter 236

A few minutes later, I heard a scuffling in the back.

I walked to the kitchen to find Derry and Kelly just coming in the back door.

"Glad you made it," I said smiling. I went and closed the door behind them. As I closed it, I looked out, seeing a face disappear behind the fence.

"We went to the Home to check on Johnny," said Derry.

"I got your note," I said.

"I knew you wouldn't want me to, but I just had to go over," said Derry.

"It's fine," I said, "I understand why you went and it's fine. It's good. You did your work."

I explained that I had met with Heirpat at the jail.

308

"What now? You can't go in there with a squirt gun or your cane. What now?"

"We'll just wait now for Heirpat to come to us."

"So what do we do next?" asked Derry.

"Lunch," I said.

Chapter 237

As we sat, Derry and I eating salads as Kelly scarfed down a couple of hot dogs bloody with ketchup, I asked about something on my mind.

"Derry, do you still have the feeling you'll lose someone soon?" I asked.

Derry put down her fork. She looked at me then quickly to Kelly.

"Yes."

"Derry," I said. I cleared my throat about to speak the impossible. "Derry, you could run. You could leave, and I could stay here to protect the boy. You would be safe, he would never come after you. And I can wait to end it here. You could survive."

"It's never been a question of my survival, not in the past, not now."

"What about you?" said Derry pointedly. "Why don't you leave?"

"It's my job," I said.

"Well, it's mine, too. And it's more than a job, and you know that, don't you? You mean more than that to me, and to Kelly. And we're in this together."

"You don't have to be," I said.

"I've chosen you. And that's that," snapped Derry.

Kelly had put down his bread sloppy with red sauce and meat.

I looked a long time at Derry. She had chosen me.

I looked to Kelly's inquiring face.

"Hotdog," I said.

Chapter 238

It's obvious to monsters of my calibre that humans see so much of their lives through the very shallow lens of mating. And this unconscious scanning of the world for suitable mates creates endless hideous consequences among simple social relationships. Jew and Gentile, black and white, straight and gay, beautiful and ugly, fat, thin, balding, glasses, freckles, kinky hair, body hair in general, age, intelligence, riches, big breasts, strength and athleticism—humans use millions of yardsticks to measure their fellows for suitability, heap endless judgments upon each other, judgments based on the subtle unconscious search for acceptability for procreation. And how freely they let these lion-clawed judgments rip flesh from unsuspecting others. Odd that a vampire like myself would even care. You see, for a vampire, basically everybody is on the menu.

Chapter 239

We spent the rest of the afternoon occupied with small household tasks and entertainments. I watched cartoons with Kelly a bit. Then we watched the news. Derry read Kelly a story. I read Kelly a story. Kelly played with toys as Derry and I talked.

We three fixed a chicken dinner feast, dressing up Kelly in an apron and letting him flip the frying meat from a chair.

It was surprising how fast the hours past.

At one point Kelly found a small moving black spider walking the rug.

"Just a second," I said. And I took a tissue and carefully dropped the tiny monster out of doors. I remembered as a kid once I'd seen my grandfather pick one up in his bare hand, uncaring.

"You're funny, always offering your eternal protection," said Derry amused. She came and put a palm on my elbow.

"And what about you, offering love to a vampire," I said.

Without blinking Derry said, "No limits."

Chapter 240

Sitting in the window, I spent the entire night looking down on the dark street. I didn't see any unnoticed black shadows moving one way or another. Oddly, as I sat with the thinnest moonlight falling behind in the kitchen, I could almost make out my reflection.

Chapter 241

The next day was uneventful until Derry approached me with slight trepidation.

"Bill, I have something for you. I, I hope you'll understand," she said.

Derry held out a small vial with a small spot of red liquid.

"I asked Kelly and he said yes," she said looking at me earnestly.

I'm a sucker for pleading eyes.

Derry was offering me a bit of her son's blood.

"Please, Bill, take it. If it will cure you, take it for us," she pleaded.

"I would lose my powers," I said evasively.

"We don't care, we want you among us."

I looked down and swallowed. I didn't want curing at the expense of the young. Besides it was too late for that.

"Derry, please, understand this. It wouldn't do any good. You see, I am very very old."

"How old?" she asked, her hand with the vial lowering.

"Centuries, Derry."

Derry looked down and nodded.

Then wiped at a tear.

Then left the room.

Chapter 242

Amid the siege, Derry occupied herself with Kelly, entertaining him with board games and storytelling. I had listened sitting against my wall. Weary with experience, at least the small events of home life were a comfort to watch.

Every once in a while Derry would cast an eye my way. And smile. And go back to her entertainments and chores. I suppose telling me I too was a part of this, in whatever shallow way I participated. I felt I was a part.

I even tried my hand at Monopoly. But the sum of my property amounted to Baltic Avenue and Boardwalk. Two assets I could not seem to put together.

"Go directly to jail, do not pass go!" shouted Kelly before I picked up a card from Chance.

I cocked an eye as I read the card then looked at Derry.

Kelly had his mother's ESP.

I put my token in jail.

"Sorry, Kelly, jail's a place I'm comfortable with. Time to end this game, son."

Derry was looking at me strangely as she put her arm around Kelly's shoulder. Then I excused myself, much to Kelly's disappointment and upset protests.

I left the room to go sit by my window.

I opened it and leaned out. It was a night sky greatly speckled with stars. A great map upon which no one had traced the ways.

Chapter 244

I heard another enter the room.

"So, what is missing for you?" asked Derry behind me in the darkness.

I didn't turn from my window.

As a vampire, I was helpless to say. I shook my head in silence.

I felt a hand fall upon my shoulder.

I turned to her.

"Come to me," she said.

Then she threw her arms around my neck, pulling my face down, and kissed me. Kissed me with a vengence.

"You can't drill love into me," I said. I didn't know if I felt amusement or despair. "If it isn't there, it isn't."

"No don't say that. Love heals, love returns," said Derry.

At that, had I been human, I supposed I would have cried. I heard Kelly calling for his mother somewhere across the house.

I merely shook my head.

"Like so many, you think love is the answer to everything," I said.

"Love is not an answer, it's a method," replied Derry.

"So there is method to your madness," I said dismissively.

Derry pushed away and shouted.

"And none to yours!"

I stood waxen before her. Then Derry laughed.

Then she cried.

I put my arm around her trembling shoulder, hoping to at least convey the feeling of comfort and compassion.

And then Derry said something wonderful.

"I will believe in love, and I don't care if it's true."

Chapter 245

The next evening Derry was in the kitchen fixing dinner as I entertained Kelly. Suddenly he got a strange look on his face and he said, "Something funny is going to happen."

"Tonight?" I asked.

"Yeah," said Kelly.

"What?" I asked.

Kelly could only shrugged.

I walked Kelly upstairs. Then I took a plastic bag from my pocket. In it was his water flower.

Kelly reached for the squirt flower eagerly.

"I want you to wear this tonight," I said. "But whatever you do don't squirt me, okay? We'll play a joke on your Mom, but just wait until I say. Okay?" I said.

Kelly nodded eagerly, already fretting at his shirt cuff putting on the toy.

Chapter 246

I wondered when and where Heirpat would attack. I made preparations, filling the Big Squirt 2000 and my trusty orange squirt gun holstered under my arm.

The clock was tolling 12 when I noticed Derry looking at me.

Her expression was grave.

"There's evil in our backyard," she said.

Chapter 247

Derry and I quickly hurried through the house to the backdoor. As I looked out into the blackness, I saw figures coming over the fence. All told, there looked to be about ten of them climbing into the backyard.

"I'll take care of this," I said to Derry, "Take Kelly upstairs and lock yourself in."

Derry nodded and left as I placed my cane down against the door sill. I put on plastic gloves from my pocket, then picked up the Big Squirt 2000 from where I'd stowed it in the kitchen sink.

I began pumping it up furiously.

When I was sure the pressure was up, I opened the back door and stepped out. There was a lot of rustling in the dark as I appeared on the back porch, my deadly watergun pointed ahead of me like a water wand witching for vampires.

They were big burly ones. About nine or ten men standing around the yard in a half-circle where they'd dropped over the fence. Unshaven faces, grim and troll-like, were watching me with anticipation. They began stepping my way.

The quarters were a little close. I was going to have to be careful about not getting splashed.

I took a deep breath and jogged quickly around the backyard, squirting a fine string of vampire de-icer into each surprised face as I went by. It took me about 7 seconds to make the sweep.

When I turned around on the porch again, they were all still standing.

"Heirpat said this asshole may do that," one of them grunted, "Now let's just kick his ass."

I realized they weren't vampires. They were humans. Ten of them closing in on me.

And I was in for a fight.

The first thing I did was throw my Big Squirt 2000 and my little orange squirt gun as far over the fence as I could.

Chapter 248

One of them grabbed my arm and I smashed his face and I hoped it drove his nose into his brain. I kicked another one in the groin so hard he lofted then fell flat on his back. I jumped, took one by the head, and broke his neck. I caught another by the collar and hair and started shaking his head like a maraca. These humans began to back off realizing I was good.

Then I heard Derry scream from within the house.

I realized I'd been had.

Chapter 249

I dropped my maraca victim and rushed into the house. I picked up my cane on the way through the kitchen, then clambered up the stairs to the second story bedrooms. I had heard another scream from Derry on the way up. I grasped my cane a little harder as I bound up the stairs.

"Stop! Or I kill your human."

Heirpat was standing in front of the bedroom door holding Derry, one hand on the top of her head the other on her neck as if he were about to twist the cap off a jar. Derry was kicking and unsuccessfully throwing elbows. Behind them, I saw the door was open and Kelly standing wide-eyed in the bedroom not knowing what to do.

I stopped with my foot on the top step, my hand griping my cane mid-staff ready to thrust.

"Put down the cane, Mr. Exterminator," laughed Heirpat. His eyebrows had gone up with sarcasm, his mouth forming a sneer crooked as an oyster-shell. "Of the thousands of humans whose bloodlines I've ended, this one would give me greatest pleasure just to do it before you, Cousin!"

"Don't Cousin me," I said.

"Oh, Bill, we are blood relatives are we not? Don't I have your wife and child's blood in my veins? Doesn't that make us related in the most intimate vampire way?"

Derry's face suddenly crisped with pain. She began to yelp as Heirpat squeezed the back of her neck in a vice-like crush.

I set my cane down against the wall.

"Don't kill her," I said.

"Oh, I don't want to, you know that. I just want to extinguish the other little light behind me, deny this new blood to the world. And to show you what you really want."

With that Heirpat reached to the front of Derry's nightshirt and began ripping it from her, husking her like an ear of corn. In an instant, her body was naked, shaking, and in pain before me in the grip of an aged vampire.

"Here are all your vampire desires," laughed Hierpat. With his great vampire strength, he lifted Derry by the neck until she was on tiptoes. He was showing me an example of her exposure, weakness, and humiliation. "Now leave me to mine!"

"No! No! Oh!" said Derry then her eyes rolled up and she fainted with pain. Her body slumped dangling like a marionnette.

"No deal," I said. I put my hand out to reach for the cane again.

Heirpat threw Derry at me. Her body hit my chest, knocking us both backwards. I realized I had to protect Derry as we fell down the stairs, envelope her, as we painfully bumped and rolled down. We finally hit bottom.

When I sat up Derry's body was limp across my lap, naked, abused, and unconscious. I looked down on my loved one thus in vampire misery.

Chapter 250

Heirpat was no longer at the top of the stairs.

I struggled up from under Derry in a great hurry. Though bruised, nothing of myself was broken. Once again, I clambered up the stairs, hoping I was not too late to catch Heirpat before he attacked Kelly.

"Kelly! Don't go near him!" I yelled. But I expected Kelly's fear was such that he was frozen and powerless as I'd seen many young victims be.

When I leapt to the top steps, I saw Heirpat, his cloaked back to me, bending over something in the middle of the bedroom.

I rushed through the door, grabbing his stooped shoulders to pull him back.

But at that instant the old vampire swung around in a crouch holding my cane to his stomach, and, growling, he thrust it forward with all his might.

He staked me right through the chest.

Chapter 251

I felt the silver tip of my cane burning through me. I looked down at it as Heirpat released my ancient weapon and backed away. My pain was tremendous, and all I could see was the handle of my cane, looking back at me with its laughing doggy face.

I stumbled to one knee. Then I gasped, a liquid filling my eyes I had not felt for years. My eyes had filled with tears. And I felt I needed to lie down to rest. I slumped to my side.

"Walk with a cane, die with a cane," sneered Hierpat.

"Bill! Bill! Are you all right?" I heard from Kelly's innocent voice.

I blinked and looked over at Kelly, his face a mask of fear and grave concern. I sat up. But I couldn't get to my feet. Heirpat's mouth shrivelled in disgust, dismissing me, turning once again toward Kelly.

And then I realized I was not dying. Heirpat, in his inexperience, had staked me two inches too low. He had aimed too low and missed my heart. And though I could feel the burning silver within me, my misery and piercing agony, I still was not dead.

Chapter 252

"Kelly, I'm all right," I said.

This was greeted by a snort from Heirpat as he stepped closer to his young victim.

I said through my pain and horror as calmly as I could, "Kelly, Kelly boy, don't worry about that man."

And as Kelly looked helplessly at me, I winked.

"Why don't you show him that flower of yours?"

Kelly looked over at me and I saw it dawn on his face what I meant.

"Yes, Kelly, let me take a close look at that flower there," said Hierpat as he lowered his face toward the boy's chest to strike.

And as Heirpat suddenly bared his fangs and grabbed the boy, Kelly did what he should.

He squirted the old vampire right in the face and laughed.

Chapter 253

Hierpat didn't laugh. He went wide-eyed with shock.

Then he literally exploded into ragged pieces and a cloud of dust. It was like somebody blew up and harshly popped a big old vaccum cleaner bag.

Man, I'd never seen an old crappy vampire do that!

Chapter 254

Kelly looked over at me surprised and bewildered as if a party balloon had just burst in front of him.

"Gosh," said Kelly.

"Nice shot," I said.

I grinned.
Kelly grinned.

Then we both laughed.

Chapter 255

I turned my back and pulled the cane from my chest. It was painful and ugly like the regurgitation of a dog, and I didn't want Kelly to see it.

"There we go, Kelly," I said over my shoulder, "We're okay now."

I sat a minute, trying to catch my breath. I felt a little pity for my former vampire victims. Man, this hurt.

Then there was a commotion at the bedroom door. Derry, still naked and bruised, her hair disheveled and flying in wisps, rushed into the room on bare feet.

She looked from me on the floor then to Kelly and rushed to grab up the boy. She fell to the floor, sitting and clutching him to her bare chest.

"Oh, Kelly, Kelly," she said crying and rocking him.

"We're okay, Momma," said Kelly earnestly.

"I am, too," I said, sitting up feeling the burning hole of a staked vampire running through me.

I guess you could say that was a lie.

Chapter 256

Derry continued to weep clutching Kelly to her.

"It's okay, Derry," I said, "That vampire is gone, he'll never come after you again. You're safe."

Derry shuddered and took a deep breath. She began to look around, seeing me sitting on the floor. Still holding Kelly against her, she scooted across the floor to me.

"He's gone," I said. I still wasn't doing well.

"Are you all right?" Derry asked. I felt her hand upon my shoulder.

"Oh, no," I said, "I'm still a vampire."

I tried to smile, but not with much luck.

"At least it's over," I said.

Derry looked at me. I could feel she was checking her psychic inventory.

She shook her head.

"No, Bill! I still feel it. I feel I'm going to lose someone."

How did she know I wondered.

"Derry, you're okay, your family is okay. Let Kelly's brother share a bit of his blood and he will be cured. You are safe. Now, I'm done here, it's time for me to go."

"Please, Bill, stay with us, be with our family."

I shook my head. You can't keep a vampire in the family. There was nothing left but for me to deal deep inside with my pain.

I reached inside my coat pocket and found the little glass vial I always carried. I heard Derry catch her breath as she saw it. Barehanded, I popped the little plastic stopper from its throat and then drank the contents.

All it held was a few child's tears.

Chapter 257

And then my pain was great.

As I fell to the floor dying, feeling the acid burn of a child's tears in my throat, I lay back and felt Derry bend over me and her lips pressed against my forehead.

Derry's Vampire

Epilogue

A few days later, Derry received a letter in the mail. It simply said, "A last poem from me:"

Sunset Lilacs

-for Derry

The sunset lilacs reach ever higher

with their spidery souls

we are unknowable

check the hand book of God

you are there

among the gypsy red and yellow tulips

looking up to gulp the rain

you are there in the rusty old bathtub put out to pasture

which now only the horses look down in

when you are sick you cough with the

hoarse caw of the crow to the empty wind

but you are still there, in the book

your shallow roots spread like newspapers

across sacred ground

your waiting fingers raised forever to heaven like broom handles

Derry's Vampire

in a broom closet

though you stand in lines as soldierly as fence posts

I know you'd welcome the birds come to

sit on your shoulders

you of the laugh like rising flocks of pigeons

you the fool, you the carnivore turned vegetarian

you the child of the ever-giving rainbow prism

set glow your heart

Check the handbook of God

you are there

I have written your name on every last page

So we who check the handbook

will always find you